The
Paradox
Cafe

• FOR •

Derrill

CHAPTER 1

Bud Shumway pushed in the clutch with his left foot, touched the brake with his right, and slowly shifted his tan 1975 Toyota FJ40 down into second so the engine would hold him back as he carefully wound down the long steep grade into the Paradox Valley of southwest Colorado.

He had the urge to fiddle with the ends of his mustache on the way down but managed not to, keeping both hands on the steering wheel, which was a bit too stiff for one-handed driving down steep switchbacks like this.

He watched the road carefully, not wanting to end up like his Uncle Junior, who had years ago run off the side and landed in the hospital with a broken leg. And he'd gotten off lucky with that, thought Bud, noting the rusted-out hulk of Junior's old green pickup still lying far below, now so entangled with thick scrub oak that you wouldn't know it was there unless you already knew.

The road finally eased up as Bud reached the bottom of the grade into the valley, and he now began fiddling with his mustache with his left hand while steering with his right.

Just recently, Bud's wife, Wilma Jean, had declared him cured of his fiddling habit, and Bud had finally removed the earpost in his left ear and let the piercing grow back.

She was sure that her plan of making him pierce his ear had worked, since fiddling with an earring was embarrassing enough to make him eventually quit the habit—or something like that.

But what she didn't know was that, no matter how hard she tried, he would never be completely cured and was now growing a mustache just so he had something new to fiddle with. If he didn't have something to fiddle with, he couldn't think properly, thought Bud, and he sure needed all the help he could get in that department.

He had plans for growing a long handlebar stash, the kind the old-time cowboys had, one he could say he was training as he fiddled with it. Wilma Jean had always wanted him to grow a mustache—she said it would make him even more handsome than he already was, and he was way ahead of her this time. And to make things even better, it was turning out to be a red mustache, thanks to his Scots-Irish grandpa, who'd had red hair.

The highway now straightened out and became as flat as any road in Kansas, heading dead-on through the sagebrush stands and grasslands in the valley. Bud slowed for a moment to avoid hitting a small prairie falcon as it rose from the highway with a tiny mouse in its claws.

It had been a dry winter, so the only snow Bud could see was high on the ramparts of the Uncompahgre Plateau, a good mile in altitude above the valley floor, which was itself nearly a mile high. The plateau had once been home to the Ute Indians, and Uncompahgre supposedly meant "red water." Bud had been up on the plateau a few times, but had never seen any red water, so he suspected it referred to a spring up there somewhere.

The Paradox Valley was what geographers called high desert, which meant it got hot in the summer and cold in the winter, with very little moisture during either season. That made it good for growing sagebrush and not much else, unless one had irrigation water, then you could grow some rich alfalfa hay, which was the only economy the valley had—hay and the cattle that ate it—and the numerous birds that loved the remote and wild habitat.

Bud now pushed the old FJ up to its top speed, about 60, wanting to get to his uncle's store before dark. He wondered what Uncle Junior had meant when he'd called and asked if Bud could come over from Green River for a few days.

When Bud had asked why, Junior had said there was trouble in the valley and he knew Bud could figure out who was behind it if anybody could, since Bud was a top-notch lawman.

This had been a real compliment to Bud, as Uncle Junior had been in a few minor scrapes with the law long ago when he was a hobo and rode the rails and had never really seemed to approve of Bud being in law enforcement.

Junior was Bud's uncle on his mom's side and had never much liked his sis marrying Bud's dad, who was the son of a sheriff, that grandpa that was responsible for Bud's stash being red. Bud's mom had been an O'Connor, so maybe she'd contributed to that red in his stash, too, he mused.

Bud's dad hadn't gone into law enforcement and had instead worked the uranium mines, which had eventually also become Junior's occupation after he quit riding the rails, so peace had gradually been restored.

Bud had also worked in the mines, just like his dad, but after his mining accident he'd followed in his grandpa's footsteps and become Sheriff of Emery County, where he and Wilma Jean had bought a nice little bungalow on a couple of acres on the edge of the town of Green River.

By then, Junior had seemed to be more accepting of things, maybe because his scrapes with the law had become distant memories of the past. He hadn't ridden the rails for many years at that point, having for some reason chosen to settle down in the remote Paradox Valley, where he ran the old general store.

Bud was now as far from law enforcement as one could get, working as a melon farmer. He loved the peace and quiet farming provided, lots of time to fiddle and think, and he also pretty much enjoyed having the winters off to help Wilma Jean with her cafe and bowling alley, though he had to admit his cooking could use a little help. But he had really enjoyed this past winter, it being the first he'd ever had off.

But now Uncle Junior was talking about trouble, and he hadn't wanted to elaborate, as it was a long-distance call, and could Bud just come on over for a few days? Bud had said sure he could, and now here he was, at the door of his uncle's old general store, the only business in the valley other than the one across the street, the old rickety Paradox Cafe.

Bud noted the cafe seemed to be empty, even though it was dinner time and the flashing neon sign was on. He parked his FJ in front of the old general store and went in, the screen door slamming behind him.

Bud looked around a bit, then sat down on one of the old stools at the historic but now defunct soda fountain, the first and only one in town. He started whistling the tune from an old TV show—he couldn't remember what it was from, maybe Bonanza—hoping Junior was in the back of the store and would hear him and come out.

That didn't get any results, so he sat there for a bit, then called out Junior's name, thinking he'd maybe gone to his apartment upstairs for a minute. Bud then got up and walked over to the counter and studied the various pieces of memorabilia under the glass.

One in particular struck him—it was the words to Roger Miller's song, "King of the Road." Since it was a song about hobos, Bud could understand why it appealed to Uncle Junior enough that he'd put the sheet music under the glass there. In fact, Bud had really liked that song when he was a kid, and it had been a big hit. He started humming the tune, then wailed out:

"King of the roaaaad."

He now started singing the lyrics, and by the time he got to the end, he was belting the song out, really enjoying himself, kind of half-forgetting where he was and why. He'd kind of forgotten all about that song, and it was reminding him of some good times as a kid.

But when he stopped, he noticed the singing seemed to continue on without him, the word "road" still hanging in the air.

This was a bit perplexing, to say the least. Maybe the room had some kind of strange acoustics, thought Bud, since it had the high tin ceiling that characterized these old stores. He tried it again:

"King of the roaaaad."

He stopped and listened. Sure enough, the sound continued on, but now it seemed to kind of be coming from down one of the aisles over by the ice-cream cooler with an Eskimo Pie sign on its lid. The sound soon stopped.

Now Bud had moved from perplexed to worried, and he stood, patted the shoulder holster where he always carried his Ruger, then slowly walked over to where the sound had originated.

Slowly, he stuck his head around the corner, looking down the aisle. What he saw didn't set too well with him— it was a body, and it appeared to be the body of his Uncle Junior, though he couldn't quite tell, as the face was to the floor, but it had the signature red-white-and-blue-striped American flag suspenders that Junior always wore.

Bud rushed to the man's side, carefully turning him over—sure enough, it was Junior. Just then, he heard the sound he'd heard before. Junior was moaning in the exact same key Bud had been singing in. He must've heard Bud, he thought, glad his uncle was still alive.

He helped Junior sit up, noting a large swollen lump on his forehead. Junior groaned and opened his eyes.

It certainly looked to Bud that his uncle had been right—there was indeed trouble in the Paradox Valley.

CHAPTER 2

Bud helped Junior stand up, then half-carried him over to the corner, easing him into a big worn easy chair near the wood stove. Junior had lost one of his run-down moccasins, so Bud retrieved it and put it back on his foot, noting the cuffs of Junior's Wrangler jeans were in tatters where they dragged on the ground. It apparently wouldn't hurt Junior to hitch his suspenders up a notch, Bud noted, though he suspected they were already as hitched up as could be, as his uncle wasn't very tall.

Everyone else in the area wore Levis, since that was what real cowboys wore, but not Junior. He wore Wranglers—Wranglers way too big for him and that hung so low on his skinny hips and up under his pot belly that they looked like they would fall off any minute. Junior always said he wouldn't be caught dead looking like some scraggly ignorant cowboy. And his old run-down moccasins punctuated the point.

Now Junior groaned and rubbed his head while Bud took his pulse and looked for signs of shock. Bud had plenty of experience with the injured—too much, he thought—from when he'd been a lawman.

Junior now managed to stop groaning enough to talk. He was having trouble getting the words out.

"Buddy, we need to get out of here, that wild man's still around."

"Is that who hit you, a wild man?" Bud asked.

"I think so, though I didn't see him for sure, just his shadow. Buddy, he's still in here, let's git."

With that, Junior frantically struggled to his feet and shuffled off, Bud following behind, catching him just as he almost fell out the door.

Junior was resolute and pulled Bud along, on across the street and into the Paradox Cafe, where he collapsed into a cracked orange faux-leather booth.

The place appeared to be empty, but a waitress soon emerged from the kitchen. She was small and wiry and redheaded, and Bud thought she was kind of the female equivalent of Junior, before he lost his hair, anyway. She wore a name tag that read "LuAnn."

When she saw Junior, she asked, "Oh my gosh, Junior, what happened?"

"Now, LuAnn, don't start in," Junior replied somewhat testily. "I'm OK."

"Can you keep an eye on him?" Bud asked. "Maybe put some ice on that lump? I need to go back to the store."

"No, Buddy, you stay outta there," Junior cautioned. "That wild man's still in there. He'll whack you next."

"Oh my gosh, is that what happened?" LuAnn was beside herself. "I didn't know he came down here, right into town. Somebody better call the sheriff."

"It'll take them an hour to get here, and he'll be long gone by then," Junior replied, referring to the fact that the nearest sheriff's office was in the next county.

"Now, my lil' Junior-bug, let me get you somethin' to drink," LuAnn offered, worried. "You OK?"

"You ain't got the kinda drink I need," Junior replied. "And I ain't your damn Junior-bug or June-bug or nuthin', Loony Ann. You're making me sicker than I was before. Say, Bud, if you're going back to the store, get me my..."

But he was too late, Bud was long gone.

•   •   •

Bud stood outside, just around the corner of the store, trying to get a look in through the front window. His hand was on his Ruger, no longer in its holster but instead in his jacket pocket where he could keep his finger on the trigger.

He was trying to remember if he'd seen his uncle turn off the lights, because they were now definitely out. He knew he himself hadn't turned them off, as he didn't even know where the switch was.

But now the lights were off, and it was dark enough that he couldn't really see much inside. And he sure as heck wasn't about to put himself in danger by going inside and looking around for the light switch, Bud mused.

He stood there, listening, then decided to go around and check the back. He hadn't been to his uncle's store for a good six or seven years, when he and Wilma Jean lived over in Radium, an hour away in the direction of the switchbacks he'd just come down. He couldn't remember what was in the back of the store, but he was pretty sure the building had to have a back door.

Bud was already regretting coming to Paradox, though he was glad he was able to help his uncle. The last thing he wanted was to get back into law enforcement, and this was already beginning to have that feel to it.

He snuck down the side of the building, ducking down when he passed a window, then carefully trying to peek into it. But it was too dark to see anything, so he crept further along the side, then looked around the back corner.

Sure enough, there was a back door with its dim porch light on, and next to it sat a couple of old rusted-out 50-gallon oil drums, the kind you could carry in the back of your pickup, relics of the old uranium era, which had been in full swing here in Paradox just like over the hill in Radium. Junior must be using them as burn barrels, thought Bud, from the burned sooty look of the rims and the smell of ashes.

Now Bud saw the door slowly push open from the inside, and he pulled back a bit around the corner, not wanting to be seen. He could now see someone coming through, even though it was too dark and shadowy to make out much.

They stepped outside, and Bud could tell they were worried about being seen, as they hunched down and snuck down along the old barrels, trying to stay hidden.

Bud pulled his Ruger from his pocket, wondering if he were legal to carry concealed in Colorado. He knew he was OK in Utah, but he couldn't recall if the two states had a mutual agreement to honor each other's licensing. He smiled kind of wryly at himself for worrying about such things when his life could be in danger.

Just then, whoever it was decided to go for it and began running. Bud almost dropped his gun in shock. Whoever it was, they were a good foot taller than he was, and he was over six-feet tall. And they were huge, built like a linebacker, nobody Bud would want to tangle with.

Bud had planned to fire a few warning shots, but seeing the size of who he was dealing with, all he wanted at that point was for them to keep running.

He returned his gun to its holster, stood and watched for a moment to make sure they were gone, then turned and slowly walked back across the street to the Paradox Cafe, feeling a bit like he was in a dream.

CHAPTER 3

"It wasn't a wild man, it was a Bigfoot," said LuAnn, leaning against the back of the booth where Bud and Junior sat.

"I've never seen no Bigfoot skulk around and try to hide like Bud described," answered Junior. "They're big and go wherever they want, no need to skulk. They adhere to the adage that it's better to ask forgiveness than permission, though I couldn't picture one asking for forgiveness, either."

"Can I take it that you've seen a Bigfoot then?" Bud grinned.

"I didn't say that, Buddy, and if I had, I sure wouldn't want the town reporter here to know," Junior answered.

LuAnn laughed good-naturedly and started to whack Junior on the head with a menu, then stopped, remembering he'd already been whacked pretty good over at the store.

"Yup, my little Junior Mint, I do keep track of everything that's going on here in this little worthless town, and you'd better remember that. You boys want something to eat before I close?"

Bud studied the menu, then ordered a chicken-fried steak. Junior said, "I'll have Adam and Eve on a raft, and wreck 'em."

As LuAnn disappeared into the kitchen, Junior smiled at the quizzical look on Bud's face.

"That's hobo talk for two fried eggs on toast, and wreck 'em means scramble them. If you don't want them scrambled, you say you want 'em with their eyes open. LuAnn knows what I mean—she's been around me way too long."

Bud grinned, suddenly wishing he himself had been able to spend more time with his uncle.

"You feeling OK?" Bud asked.

"I'm OK. Didn't even knock me out. Just feel a little headachy."

"What exactly happened?"

"I dunno. I was back putting some price tags on some cans and I heard somebody come in. I yelled out that I'd be there in a minute, then I heard somebody really heavy come back to where I was. I knew it was somebody heavy by the way the floor boards squeaked.

Just as I turned, somebody hit me on the head. I didn't black out, though I did fall pretty hard, but I managed to see a shadow, and it looked like the wild man. I rolled over and played dead until I heard somebody singing 'King of the Road,' who I figured was you. You were a little off-key, by the way, kind of sharp."

"You ever actually seen the wild man? Who is he, anyway?"

"Naw, I never seen him, but it looked like the description I've heard. He's this big guy who lives up on the Uncompahgre and scares the hell out of anybody who goes near his territory. A number of hunters have seen him, and he steals their food, hell, even their game. He's supposed to be half Bigfoot and half human, but I dunno about that. But he's one big hombre."

"Well, I can attest to that," agreed Bud, still feeling a bit shaky from the encounter. "But why would he come into town—has he ever done that before?"

"Not until recently," Junior replied. "Not until that damn son of a biscuit Mack Murphy came around trying to buy everybody out so he could own the whole damn valley all by himself. He even tried to buy me out..."

Junior now paused mid-sentence, reflecting, chewing on a toothpick he'd pulled from his shirt pocket. He then slowly continued, "...and said if I didn't sell, he couldn't guarantee my continuing good health."

Junior was now turning a deep shade of red. He finally spat out the toothpick and said, "Now I know what's going on, Buddy, my boy, now I know. Mack sent the wild man to pay me a visit, that sumsagun. I have half a mind to go pay him one myself. This is why I called you over, cause Mack went too far, threatening me, and now getting me whacked on the head. If you hadn't showed up when you did, who knows..." His voice trailed off just as LuAnn brought their dinner.

"You sure you feel good enough to eat this, Junior?" she asked. "I can get you a takeout box — you look kind of red, like you're maybe a bit short of breath."

She looked imploringly at Bud, as if asking him if things would be OK. She then added, "And I'm totally scared to walk home now, after all this." LuAnn had apparently been doing some thinking while cooking their dinner.

"It's OK, I can drive you home, LuAnn," Bud assured her. "You live alone?"

"I do, and I'm scared stiff. I wish I had somebody around. Maybe you and Junior would be safer over at my place. What if the wild man comes back to the store looking for you?"

"He'll be real sorry," Junior mumbled through a mouthful of eggs and toast. "But don't worry, he won't bother you."

"How do you know that?" she asked.

"Cause you already sold out," Junior answered.

CHAPTER 4

Bud and Junior had taken LuAnn home, where she elected to get her overnight stuff and go stay with her cousin, so they then ran her over to the other side of town. But since the town of Paradox had maybe 200 people at the most, that didn't take long.

When they returned, they checked out the old general store, but nothing appeared to be damaged or stolen, although Junior found an empty can of Dinty Moore beef stew on the back-room floor.

After locking the doors, they were now settled in the little apartment above the store, where Bud was trying to get comfortable sleeping on Junior's old hide-a-bed couch, which appeared to no longer have any working springs, if it ever did. Bud kept tilting like he was going to roll off.

Junior had gone straight to bed, complaining of a headache, and Bud had given him a painkiller from the emergency medical kit he kept in his FJ. This seemed to have pretty much knocked Junior out, and Bud was almost wishing he'd taken one himself. It was now almost 2 a.m., and he still couldn't get to sleep.

He pulled his sleeping bag up over his head and tried one more time to forget the image of the wild man that seemed stuck in his brain. For some reason, it was bringing back recollections of the Ghost Rock Cafe over near Green River, and he didn't like that one bit, as that was one case he preferred to forget—it had led to his quitting law enforcement. And here he was in what was looking to be a similar situation.

He wondered how Wilma Jean and their dogs, Hoppie and Pierre, were doing without him. He could picture it now—the little dachshund and the Basset hound down under the covers sleeping at Wilma Jean's feet.

Actually, now that he thought of it, they were probably sleeping under the covers on his side of the bed, little heads on his pillow, luxuriating in his absence, not missing him one bit. Pierre was probably twitching and whining, chasing rabbits in his sleep while Hoppie dreamed he was starring in some Scooby Doo episode.

Bud tried to turn over and once again nearly rolled off the edge of the couch. It tilted and was hard as a rock. He tried sleeping on his back, stretching his feet out, but the couch was too short.

He finally got up and got some Tums from his pack. That chicken-fried steak wasn't setting too well and was maybe part of the problem, he thought. LuAnn was a good enough cook, but nobody could beat Wilma Jean's chicken-fried steak back home.

He went into the kitchen for a glass of water, then stood looking out the window. For awhile, he watched a nighthawk swoop after insects, then suddenly, he thought he saw movement down on the street below.

The little town of Paradox didn't have streetlights, and instead, people left their porch lights on, including LuAnn over at the cafe. As he stood there, the cafe porch light darkened for a second as if something big had passed in front of it.

Now Bud was wide awake, carefully watching, a bit chilled. He hadn't bothered to turn the light on in the kitchen, so he knew he couldn't be seen. He strained to see more, but it was too dark. He began to slowly twist the ends of his fledging mustache.

It now appeared that whatever had passed in front of the light was directly below him, and he could barely make out a motion that resembled something going up and down, up and down, over and over. What the heck, he thought, just as the sounds of an engine drifted up to the room. He carefully and quietly opened the window an inch or so, and sure enough, something mechanical was passing below, making a kind of lurching sound.

Now it was directly in front of the general store, and the store's porch light briefly lit it up—it was a backhoe! For a moment, Bud could make out its lifted bucket, bobbing up and down a bit as the hoe drove down the street. It appeared to be carrying something, but Bud wasn't quite sure.

The backhoe lurched on down the street, turning onto the road next to the store that led down to the Dolores River. Bud knew the road dead-ended there. Its only purpose was to serve the raft take-out, as one couldn't really raft the river below that point without running into fences built by ranchers partway across the small shallow river.

Bud wanted to wake Junior and ask him why a backhoe would be going down to the river at this time of night, but he didn't want to disturb the old guy's sleep, and he knew Junior wouldn't know any more than he himself did, which was nothing. He probably wouldn't wake up anyway.

Bud toyed with the idea of following, but wasn't too keen on being out alone at night after his encounter with the wild man or whatever it had been, so he went back to the couch and lay down, trying once again to get comfortable.

But it was no use, he just couldn't sleep. He tossed and turned, then looked at his watch. It was now almost 4 a.m., and it wouldn't be long before the sun rose. He decided he might as well get up, make some coffee, and at the very least read a book or something. No point lying there miserable any longer.

He got up, got dressed, and went back into the kitchen, this time turning on the light, checking around to see where Junior kept his coffee making gear, but he couldn't even find a coffeepot, yet alone actual coffee. All he could find were a couple of old teabags with labels that looked like they were from the 1950s. Maybe Junior was keeping them to put with the other old collectible stuff on display in the store.

Dang, Bud thought, he sure needed some coffee. He decided to go out to his FJ, where he always kept a little plastic tub with a bag of coffee and some canned milk—his emergency stash, as he called it. He also had a little pan, a cup, and a one-burner portable propane stove, so he could stop by the side of the road and have coffee any time he wanted, which he often did. At such times he would sit on the FJ bumper thinking about addictions as he sipped and savored the black brew.

Now, he carefully crept down the stairs into the store, flipping on the lights. Junior surely sold coffee and cream, he thought, thinking he'd save himself from having to unlock the store to go outside to his FJ.

But all he could find was some Folgers in a five-pound can, and there was no way he was going to drink that, especially not five pounds of it, and he knew he'd have to pay Junior for it. And the only cream Junior sold was some powdered creamer that said it tasted like French Vanilla and was inspired by the cafes of Paris, whatever the hell that meant. Bud had never been to Paris, but he knew they let dogs in the cafes there, so, as much as he loved dogs, he decided to pass on that one.

Bud kind of laughed at himself, thinking back to a time when he would've been happy with Folgers. Wilma Jean had kind of helped turn him into a coffee snob, as all she would drink was freshly roasted organic coffee sent direct from some gourmet free-trade company up in Salt Lake, special UPS delivery. Bud had to admit it tasted a lot better, though he had grimaced when he saw the price.

He'd have to go on outside to his FJ if he wanted real coffee, he decided, carefully unlocking the store door. He thought about LuAnn, now afraid to go outside, knowing there was a time not long ago when nobody even bothered to lock their doors in the Paradox Valley.

He turned off the store lights. He didn't want anyone to know he was up and around. He was naturally secretive like that when not sure of his environment, and it had served him well many times, both in and out of law enforcement.

Bud slipped over to his FJ, unlocked it, then opened the back and pulled out his little plastic tub. He then remembered his folded-up camp cot was also there with his camping gear, and he grabbed that, too.

He had just locked the vehicle and was getting ready to go back into the store when he noticed movement over by the cafe. Carefully slipping down behind the FJ, he set everything down and watched from the side, his heart racing. What if the wild man was back? He then realized his Ruger was in its holster on the coffee table by the couch upstairs, a realization that made him feel a bit clammy.

Someone was walking down the street by the cafe, trying not to be seen. The porch light couldn't be avoided, so when they got close, they kind of ducked down and hid their face, almost as if they knew someone might be watching. Bud now realized it wasn't the wild man, as it wasn't big enough.

The figure was tall and wearing a cowboy hat, a pretty generic figure, as figures in the shadows go, Bud thought. There was no way he could ever identify someone like that.

But once they got out of the light and back into the shadows, they straightened back up and proceeded along the road, and Bud could now see they had a slight limp. He caught just a glimpse, then the figure was gone. He wondered if it were a temporary or permanent limp.

Bud grabbed his cot and plastic coffee tub, then quickly went into the store, locking the door and hurrying upstairs. He felt naked and defenseless without his gun, even though he'd been a good-enough brawler in his youth as a uranium miner.

But that was back before he'd met Wilma Jean and been civilized, or maybe cultured was a better word, if anyone living in the Utah deserts could ever really be cultured, he thought. He'd learned to solve problems with the same kind of panache Wilma Jean used in her cooking, using his brains instead of what he called redneck logic, which usually involved not using one's brains but instead their brawn.

Wilma Jean had taught him a lot of things, one being the merits of good coffee, and for that he would never be the same, and he could never go back to his wild ways of being happy drinking Folgers, nor could he ever be happy without her.

He grinned as he made his coffee in a pan over Junior's little two-burner stove, thinking about how Wilma Jean had changed his life. He wished she were here now, or better yet, that he were over in their little bungalow in Green River, where he belonged, not skulking around sleep-deprived in the dark in the little one-horse town of Paradox, Colorado.

The coffee boiled and Bud grabbed the pan off the stove before it could run over the sides. It was a well-practiced art, knowing exactly when to grab it off the fire, an art that resulted in having to clean coffee grounds off everything if you weren't artsy enough.

He poured the black coffee into his big mug with the words "Krider Melons" on it, added some canned milk, which immediately formed a scum on the surface, then noticed an open bag of Oreos, grabbed a couple, and took the coffee and cookies back into the living room.

He unfolded and sat up his cot, put his pillow and sleeping bag on it, grabbed a copy of Zane Grey's "Riders of the Purple Sage" from Junior's library of very limited editions and settled in to read until Junior got up.

But instead, Bud promptly dropped off into a deep sleep, dreaming he was out in the Green River Desert, chasing rabbits with Pierre and Hoppie, just as the sun broke over the ruby red cliffs of the Paradox Valley.

CHAPTER 5

Bud could tell it was late. His watch said 10:15, and he usually was up by six or seven. He was still kind of groggy and could use more sleep, but something had wakened him.

He could hear someone talking in the kitchen, and it sounded like LuAnn and Junior. He sat up on the side of the cot, still in his clothes, which were now all wrinkled, and pulled on his boots.

"You need to wake him up, Junior. Isn't that why he's here, to help us out? Didn't you say he was once a cop?"

"No, not us, me. He's here to help me out."

"Why you...you selfish old rattlesnake!"

"And he wasn't no cop, he was a sheriff. Big diff. Damned good one, too, and you know what I think of most of 'em."

"So, he's here to help you out and the rest of us can just go pound sand, that right?"

"That's right. And you know what that makes you, if I'm a rattlesnake."

"I don't wanna know."

"A rattlesnake aficionado."

"You old...OK, you wanna play like that, your eatin' privileges at the Paradox Cafe are hereby revoked. What's an aficionado?"

Bud could hear Junior laughing.

"Fine by me. Not worth eatin' anyway. And your buyin' privileges at the Paradox General Store are hereby provoked."

"You mean revoked."

"That, too. Invoked. Exvoked. Unvoked. All of it."

"Well, look at this here, Junior, you rascal. Fancy gourmet coffee, right on your kitchen counter. Holdin' out on us, eh? You sell that crap in your store for everybody else while you're up here drinkin' the good stuff. You're busted."

"You know I drink tea. Must be Buddy's. Waste of money."

"Look, Junior, let's be reasonable. We all need his help, Paradox is getting dangerous. I'm afraid to be home alone."

"What's happened is now for the county sheriff to work on, LuAnn. Buddy's not gonna get caught up in any more. And now that Mack's gone, I don't think we're gonna need anybody's help. I'm sending Buddy home. This is serious business. I may go with him, now that I think of it."

"You can't leave. Who would run the store? Has anyone called the sheriff?"

"I did. Should be here in an hour, or so they said."

"You wouldn't run off on me, would you, Junior?"

"Run off on you? You bet I would."

"Why, you old sidewinder."

Bud could tell the conversation was having a little trouble getting out of first gear and gaining momentum, so he got up and walked into the kitchen.

"Good morning," he said, still half-asleep, starting another pan of coffee.

"Morning? Don't you mean afternoon?" Junior grinned.

"Didn't get much sleep on your fancy couch," Bud replied. "What's going on? Called the sheriff?"

Junior replied, "They found Mack Murphy's body in the river this morning, along with a backhoe from his ranch. Somebody apparently used the backhoe to take his body and dump it in the river, and they drove the hoe into the water, too. Probably trying to hide fingerprints and all, with it in the water. But it ain't in very deep, since the river's way down."

"Who found it?" Bud asked, thinking about what he saw last night.

"Some rafters."

"Rafters? This early in the year?"

"Yeah, I found that odd, too," said LuAnn. "It's too shallow and cold to be rafting now."

"Maybe they were camping or something," Junior said. "Or scoping it out. But they came to the store first thing and had me call it in."

"If they camped, they would've seen the backhoe come in," Bud said. "Which I did, by the way—I saw it go by at about 2 a.m. One of the many side benefits of staying up all night, you get to see crimes in progress."

Junior asked for details, which Bud gave as he deftly pulled the pan off the stove at just the right minute.

Bud then asked, "But why kill Mack? I'm still waiting for the reason why I was asked to come over here, Uncle Junior, though I'm gradually picking up bits and pieces. But I like the idea of you running me off, if I heard that right."

LuAnn replied, "You don't need to go anywhere, Bud. But tell me, does Junior have a real name? Or was he baptized Junior like he claims? You're the first of his family I've ever met to ask."

Bud laughed. "He's Angus Fergus O'Connor the Third, last I heard. Kind of catchy, isn't it?"

"You didn't need to tell her that," Junior moaned. "I been in this valley 20 years without tellin' nobody that."

"So, you're really a junior junior, huh, the third in line," LuAnn said gleefully. "Junior's junior."

"I'm sorry," Bud said, though the look on his face said otherwise.

"I'll never live this down," said Junior, giving Bud a dirty look. "Nice job. All those years wasted."

"Somebody's gotta do it," Bud grinned. "But back to Mack. Why would anyone kill him?"

"Because he's a son of a biscuit," Junior replied.

"Say, Angus Fergus, how much did he offer you for your place here, if you don't mind my askin'?" asked LuAnn.

"I do mind you askin', and I ain't answerin' to nothin' but Junior, so you can go pound more sand."

Bud sighed. He was never going to get his answer about Mack. He poured canned milk into his coffee and took a sip.

"So how do we know you didn't kill Mack?" LuAnn asked Junior. "We know you accused him of tryin' to kill you. There's a motive right there."

"Because I have an alibi," Junior answered, disgusted. "Right, Buddy?"

"I dunno, Uncle, when I was gone outside, you could've snuck out," Bud replied, teasing.

"See! I knew it, prime suspect number one, Angus Fergus O'Connor, your Honor. Would I be a witness? You betcha."

"You have to had witnessed something, you loon," Junior replied. "I was passed out up here in my bed, I don't care what my dear loyal nephew says. And I got the lump on my head to prove it."

Junior took a toothpick out of his shirt pocket and started chewing on it.

"Oh, I'm just kidding, Junior, and you know it," LuAnn said, seeing he was upset. "We all know you would never kill nobody. You boys come over to the cafe and I'll make you something to eat. And Angus, your name's safe with me, as long as you do exactly what I say."

Bud grinned. "The way you two talk, I would swear you were married."

LuAnn's face turned a deep shade of red, and Junior's wasn't far behind. Junior gave Bud a dirty look, put the toothpick back in his pocket, stood, and dutifully followed LuAnn out the door, leaving Bud still grinning.

Bud stood and started to follow them over to the Paradox Cafe, first turning the sign on the store door that said, "Open" around to read "Open, Pay at Cafe," and still wondering why anyone would want to kill some rancher named Mack Murphy.

CHAPTER 6

Bud was just opening the store door to leave when Junior's phone rang. He turned and went behind the counter, answering it.

"Yell-ow."

"Bud, that you, Hon?"

It was Wilma Jean.

"Oh man, it's good to hear your voice. I was thinking about calling you. There's no cell phone reception over here."

"Well, that explains that," she answered. "I've been trying to call your cell. I was beginning to get a bit worried. We miss you. Pierre looked for you half the night. He's worried. Here, say something to him."

Bud smiled. "Whasup, lil' Pierresee-wearsee? You bein' a good lil' boy for your mommy?" Bud now began whining into the phone.

Wilma Jean laughed. "He acts scared. He ran into the other room." She paused. "Any idea how long you're going to be over there?"

"No idea at all. There's been a murder."

"Oh my gosh." She let out a long sigh, letting Bud know what she thought of the whole deal. "I knew you shouldn't have gone over there. I hope you're not in any danger. Who was murdered?"

"Some guy Junior didn't like."

"Well, that's a shame. I hope Junior didn't do it. Hon, you be careful. And I don't like it one bit that you don't have a phone. By the way, Howie's been calling, and he says he really needs to talk to you."

Bud groaned. Howie had been his deputy when he was sheriff in Green River and had replaced Bud in theory, but not so much in practice, as he was always calling Bud for advice.

"I'll give him a call," Bud replied.

"OK, Hon, and you be careful. Call me once in awhile."

"I will," Bud replied. "I miss you. I wish I was home."

"Well, there's no reason you can't be," she said. Bud thought she sounded a bit impatient.

"What're you having for dinner?" he asked.

"Mashed potatoes, meatloaf, and a big piece of home-made cherry pie," she answered.

Bud moaned into the phone, "Dammit, all I've had to eat since I got here is a dried out chicken-fried steak."

Wilma Jean laughed. "Just teasing you, Hon, I'm actually going down to Radium to have dinner with Peggy Sue and Hum."

Now Bud moaned even louder. "At Smitty's Steak House?"

"Yup," Wilma Jean answered, laughing. "With pie a la mode for dessert."

She laughed even more, then added, "Just kidding. Actually, I'm going to stay home and have a salad, then go to the bowling leagues."

"That's better," Bud replied, noting his stomach was growling. "OK, well, I better call Howie, so you have fun tonight."

They hung up, and Bud dialed the number for the Emery County Sheriff's Office over in Green River.

"Sheriff's Office, Sheriff Howie here."

"Howdy, Sheriff, I'd like to report a missing watermelon farmer," Bud replied.

"Oh man, I hope that's not Bud Shumway. I've been trying to call him all morning," came Howie's reply. "How do you know he's missing?"

"Because I've been trying to call him all morning."

"Well, maybe he's busy or something. You can't really expect a guy to sit by...hey, is that you Sheriff? I've been trying to call you all morning."

Bud laughed. "Howie, there's no cell service over here, so I have to get to a landline to call. And for the umpteenth time, I'm not the sheriff any more, you are."

"I know that," Howie said, sounding a bit put off. "Did your wife tell you I've been calling?"

"She did," Bud replied. "What's going on?"

"You should answer your phone. What if it's an emergency or something? That's what you always told me when I was a deputy—to cover for you and answer the phone."

"I'm sorry, Howie, but there's no cell towers around. What's up?" Bud asked patiently.

"Oh man, Sheriff, wait till you hear this. You won't believe it."

Bud knew from experience that Howie was going nowhere on the information highway until he gave him a little jump start, so he asked, "What's going on?"

"It's kind of personal, Sheriff."

"Well, I sure don't want to meddle in your private affairs, Howie," Bud replied. "No need to tell me."

"No, no, I need your advice. Maureen's starting a country swing band, and she wants me to be the lead singer. Says I have just the right voice for it. She plays a mean honky tonk piano. All we need is a guitar player and a bass. And we can both dance—we do a mean boogie woogie together."

"Well, that's great, Howie, why is that a problem?"

"Well, Sheriff, how will it look to the mayor and everyone when the sheriff and his ex-wife are playing and dancing at some honky tonk? What if there's trouble?"

"They'll probably all be there listening to you guys play," replied Bud. "And if there's trouble, well, the sheriff will be right there, no need to call him. Kind of handy, I would think. I wouldn't worry about it too much. You're allowed to have a hobby or two, just like anybody else. And maybe you and Maureen should just get remarried."

"Remarried? Us? Well, that's a thought. But the sheriff having a hobby that plays the bars?"

"Howie, there are only two bars in Green River, so if you guys are playing the bars, you'll probably be out of the county and nobody will know the difference. In fact, it might give you some notoriety. You'll become the Singing Sheriff of Emery County. You can go practice at the jail where you'll have a captive audience."

"It's too far to go over to Castle Dale for that," Howie replied. "But Sheriff, what if we get famous and I end up quitting my job?"

"Well, you'll be known as the Singing Ex-Sheriff of Emery County."

"So you think it's OK?" Howie was beginning to sound excited.

"Sure, and you know old Barry Smith, he used to play bass for some jazz band back in Chicago years ago. He's that guy down at the highway shop."

"No, Bud, it's not that kind of bass, not a stand-up bass, but a bass guitar. We're gonna play stuff like old Hank Williams songs."

Before Bud could reply, Howie started singing into the phone, "Well, hey there, mister, can you spare some shoes, I wore mine out walkin' those honky tonk blues."

Bud was actually surprised at the rich mellow tone of Howie's voice. He wasn't a bad singer at all, he thought.

Howie continued, "I been practicing yodeling as I drive around in the patrol vehicle. Hope I never forget and leave the mike turned on, someone might mistake it for a 10-51, you know, driving under the influence. And Maureen says I need to learn to play the guitar, and she's gonna get me one. Say, Sheriff, you ever hear the Cherokee Boogie?"

Bud answered, "No, Howie, but this is long distance on my uncle's phone, so I better not talk much longer."

"Oh gee," Howie replied. "How long you gonna be over there? Where the heck are you, anyway?"

"In the town of Paradox, Colorado, Howie. It makes Green River look downright cosmopolitan."

"Well, thanks for the advice, Sheriff, and don't stay over there too long. They got any honky tonk bars? Put a good word in for us. We're going to call ourselves the Ramblin' Road Rangers. Say, you interested in maybe being our manager? I mean, you pretty much have the winters off, being a farmer and all."

"Well, Howie, I'll have to think about that. It might be fun, but I'm not sure Wilma Jean would approve, as I'm supposed to be helping her at the bowling alley and cafe. But I'll talk to her. You keep me posted, OK?"

"Sure. OK, gotta go, Maureen just came in. Catch you later, Sheriff. 10-4, over and out."

CHAPTER 7

Bud left the store and started to go into the Paradox Cafe, but changed his mind and got into his FJ instead. He wanted to go down to the river to see what was going on, assuming anything still was.

He suspected the sheriff would go there upon arrival, since that's where the action had been, and he was hoping to meet up with him. His stomach could wait another half-hour or so for breakfast.

Bud wished he were back in Green River. He could go have a hot roast-beef sandwich, complete with mashed potatoes, at Wilma Jean's Melon Rind Cafe, then go take a nap, with Pierre and Hoppie snoozing on his lap.

Hopefully, all this drama with his uncle would soon be over and he would be home. He was enjoying seeing the old guy but would starve to death if he had to depend on LuAnn's cooking for very long.

The Dolores River raft takeout was only a quarter mile or so from the store, and Bud passed an ambulance coming up the dirt road as he drove in, its lights flashing but no siren. Behind it drove a white pickup with a San Miguel Sheriff logo on the side. Bud slowed down and waved, hoping the sheriff would stop, but no such luck.

Bud pulled up next to the raft takeout, simply a place on the bank that had been leveled out with the sagebrush and willows removed. He could see a backhoe not too far from shore, sunk about a third of the way into the shallow river. Several Canadian geese paddled in the water nearby.

An older brown van sat nearby in the willows, and two young guys with longish hair, maybe in their early twenties, leaned on it as if waiting. One of them called out, "You with the sheriff?"

Bud parked and got out to go talk to them.

"Howdy, fellas. No, I'm not with the sheriff. But if you don't mind, I'd like to talk to you for a minute. I'm assuming you're the ones who found the body?" He handed them a card from his wallet.

They studied it, then one of them replied, "I thought you said you weren't with the sheriff. This card says you're the Sheriff of Emery County, Utah."

"It's an old card, all I have. I'm a P.I. now, private investigator."

Bud was kind of hesitant to identify himself as an investigator, but he figured he might as well try to help out his uncle and figure out what he could.

"Oh, well, investigate away, we don't know nuthin'," the kid answered.

"Could you tell me what happened, how you found the body, and exactly where it was?"

Now the other kid was talking. "We was out here early, um, lookin' for a place to put a raft in, and we saw a body over there in the tamarisk. I noticed it before Carl here did, I saw something over there. It was all hung up."

"You were out here looking at putting a raft in the water? Where's your raft? Isn't it a bit cold to be rafting?"

"Aw, just tell him the truth, Jimmy, he ain't gonna arrest us. You won't arrest us will you Mr. Shumway?"

"I can't arrest anybody. I'm not a lawman anymore," Bud answered.

"We came out here to go fishin', but we ain't got no license. But we weren't breakin' the law, cause we didn't catch nuthin', at least not with a hook, in fact, we actually just kinda rescued a few fish. We were up the river a bit, and the fishin' got too interestin' for us up there, so we came down here. That's when things got even more interestin'. We should've stayed up there." Jimmy motioned towards the backhoe.

Now Carl took over. "So we went up to the store and reported it, and the guy there said to come back down here and wait for the sheriff. But we're about to get outta here."

"What's the hurry?" Bud asked.

"It's too interestin' around here, like I said," Jimmy answered.

Bud was puzzled and not sure what to say, so he just stood there, looking at the pair.

Carl finally continued, "Look, we were up there a ways fishin', and we wasn't havin' much luck, water's too cold, I guess. Do fish hibernate? Just up around that little bend a ways. It was early, dawn almost, just a bit of daylight. We decided to come out early since we don't have a license and sometimes that's when the fish jump, though we've never tried it this soon in the season. But I was just standin' there, when a great big rainbow came floatin' down the river, floppin' like it was dyin', so I waded out and grabbed it. It looked like it had been whacked on the head, but otherwise good eatin', so I kept it."

He then opened the sliding door on the side of the van and showed Bud three large rainbow trout in what looked like a gold-sluicing pan.

Jimmy now took up the story. "This happened three times. But Carl, you forgot to tell him about the noises. We could hear what sounded like somebody throwing really big rocks into the river—kersplash!! And each time, a big trout would come floatin' down."

"Well, we were thinkin', man, this is how you fish, it don't get any better, when the guy who'd been doin' all the work came around the corner."

He paused, and Bud could see he was nervous.

Carl now took over, "He stayed over in the willows on the other side of the river, but from what we could see, he was really big and all dressed in black, so we ran like hell and jumped in the van.

About then, he started wading the river, and man, the water wasn't even hardly up to his knees. We took off and drove up to town. And we managed to leave the fish," he laughed nervously. "Scared the crap out of us."

Now Jimmy was talking, "So we decided to wait for it to get a bit lighter, then we came back and got the fish. The big black guy hadn't found them cause we'd put them up in a tree where the coyotes wouldn't get them."

"There were coyotes, too?" Bud asked, a bit incredulously.

"A whole pack was sittin' on the other side of the river, watchin' us. Gave me the heebie jeebies. So we grabbed the fish and moved, came down to this stretch of river, but we talked about it and decided to call it a day and not press our luck. That's when we saw the backhoe and the body, floatin' just right there, caught in the tammies."

Bud sighed. He wasn't sure how much of the story to believe. A pack of coyotes? A big man dressed in black killing fish by throwing rocks into the river?

As if he could read his mind, Carl said, "Look, come over here if you don't believe us." He led Bud to the edge of the river a few feet from the takeout and pointed to the ground.

There, sunk deep into the mud, were two large footprints that looked like the print of a barefoot man. A very large barefoot man.

Bud went back and got his camera from the FJ and went back to take photos. He then asked, "Were you here when the ambulance came?"

"No," answered Carl. "We drove back over to the store to get something for breakfast, but there was nobody there."

"I passed the ambulance and the sheriff coming out as I was coming in. You had to have been here. Are you sure you didn't see them?" Bud asked.

Jimmy answered, "We saw the sheriff, but we just figured we'd get in trouble, so we kinda hid, to be honest. He could see the body same as we did. He busted us here fishing once before. We did our good citizenly duty—we called in the report, no need to press our luck."

"You guys have a phone or something where I can get in touch with you if I need to?"

"No," Carl answered warily. "We live over in Naturita. No phone."

Bud could tell he wasn't going to get any more information from the pair, so he let it go.

"OK, well, you boys might want to head on out. This

might not be such a good place to hang out anymore."

"No crap, Sherlock," Jimmy answered, grinning.

Carl gave Jimmy a dirty look, so Jimmy added, "Whoops, sorry, no disrespect meant."

"It's OK," Bud replied, then got into his FJ, turned around and left, but not before writing down their plates. He had a hunch the sheriff was still around and would want to know about them. He wondered why they had gold-panning gear in the back of their van.

Something about their story seemed fishy to him.

• • •

As Bud arrived back in Paradox, sure enough, the San Miguel County Sheriff's truck was parked in front of the Paradox Cafe. He parked his FJ next to it and got out.

Bud opened the door of the cafe, and the scent of fried eggs and ham hit him in the face. The place was busy, and it took him a minute to spot Junior sitting in a back booth, along with a man Bud figured must be the sheriff, who kind of looked like someone in a Zane Grey novel— lanky and tanned and wearing a gray felt cowboy hat, even though he was now indoors. Junior waved, and Bud walked back to the booth.

"Buddy, this is Sheriff Joe Walters. Joe, my nephew Bud Shumway."

The sheriff stood and held out his hand, then asked, "Any chance you know a Bud Shumway over in Utah?"

They shook hands as Bud replied, "I do, probably better than anyone else on Earth."

"So, I take it you're the same guy?" Joe asked. "I heard about that murder you solved over there in Radium, the one with the rock-shop guy."

"Yeah, that was somethin' else," Bud smiled. "Those skeletons up at the Slickrock Cafe were quite the deal."

Junior grinned, obviously proud of his nephew. "He's quite the lawman, Joe, or was, anyway. He has an honest profession now as a melon farmer."

Joe gave Junior a sideways look. "I thought you didn't much care for us lawmen types, Junior, and now I find out you've got 'em in the family."

"He ain't your ordinary lawman type, Joe, and neither are you, or I wouldn't let you set foot in my store."

"Say, Sheriff," Bud said, "I was just down with the fellows who called in the body—did you get a chance to talk to them?"

Joe looked surprised. "No, what I took to be their van was there, but they were gone. Did you get any contact info?"

"No, they wouldn't give me anything but their first names, Carl and Jimmy. But I did get their story. And their plates."

"Did they mention if they were from Naturita or not?" Joe asked.

"They said they were. You know them?"

"Yup," Joe said grimly. "They're always in and out of trouble. Mostly small stuff, but if they don't clean up their act, they're in for bigger trouble. No respect for the law. What did they tell you?"

But before Bud could answer, the door of the cafe was flung open and in rushed a tall thin blonde woman, her hair sticking out all over like straw, dressed in a long flowery dress and sandals, even though it was still chilly outside.

She began frantically yelling, "Junior in here? Junior, where are you? Junior!"

"Oh my god," Junior said, "It's that loony tune Indie, and she's lookin' for me. Quick, lemme out, I gotta hide."

But it was too late, the woman had spotted him and was soon standing by the booth, breathless and excited.

"Junior, Junior, call the sheriff!" she commanded.

Junior sighed, "You mean this guy sitting right here next to me?"

Bud was beginning to think that Junior was kind of the town center, the man everyone came to for advice and help.

The woman seemed to finally be registering that Junior wasn't alone, and that one of the men with him was indeed the sheriff.

She drew a breath, then blurted out, "I was awakened in the middle of the night by the sound of horses running past my house. I didn't think too much of it, as sometimes Annie's horses get out, but they can't go far because of the cattle guard, so I went back to sleep."

She paused for breath, then continued. "Then I later heard some kind of machinery driving by, about 1 a.m. But this morning I went over to the main house, and Annie's gone, Mack's gone, the horses are gone, and even their old dog Maggie's gone. I know something terrible's happened, Sheriff, I just know it. The cars are all there, and the saddles, too, so they didn't go riding. And the backhoe's missing. You gotta come check it out."

CHAPTER 8

Bud and Junior followed the sheriff's pickup down a dusty ranch road, that, like the highway, was straight as an arrow, cutting between large alfalfa fields. Indie, whose real name according to Junior was Indigo Jones, led the procession in her gray Honda sedan, stirring up a cloud of dust that the others had no trouble following.

"She's a real loony tune," Junior was telling Bud, "She makes LuAnn look sane."

Bud grinned, and he thought he could see a hint of red creeping up Junior's neck. "Not that I give a hotdamn about LuAnn—she's loony, too," Junior added.

"Indie sure doesn't strike me as being native to the valley. Where's she from?" Bud asked.

"Who knows?" Junior answered. "Watch it! Don't hit those chukars! Not the United States, that's for sure. She's from California or Boulder or someplace where they're so open minded their brains all fell out."

"What does she do here to make a living?"

"Not a whole lot, is my guess. She sold her place in wherever and made a killing, then bought five acres from Annie and Mack and built her a house out of straw bales, you know, the kind the big bad wolf can blow down. She's an addiction counsellor, goes over to Tellyride ever so often, has an office there, and tells the alchies and druggies how to clean up their acts. They're usually there by court order, so she has a captive audience. But I don't think she works much, even when she's supposedly working."

"Sounds like a good thing to me," Bud replied, not sure why his uncle would have a problem with her being a counsellor. He guessed the nearby ski town of Telluride had its share of problems, and anyone who could help out deserved to make a little cash, in his opinion.

"Oh, sure, it's a good thing, alright, these people need help for sure, but it's how she goes about it. She just trades one addiction for another."

"How so?"

"She fills their heads with crap, you know, like creating your own reality, attracting good things to you, all that."

"Maybe I need to have a talk with her," Bud replied, thinking of his fiddling habit.

Just then, the entourage turned under a huge log gate with an elaborate metal sign with the words "Big Mack's Little Ponderosa Ranch" etched under a cutout of a big buffalo. They then continued down a long lane between fields just beginning to green up with huge irrigation sprinklers sending out long sprays of water. In a distant field a herd of buffalo grazed.

"Big Mack's Little Ponderosa Ranch," Junior commented wryly, "with not a ponderosa in sight. Should've called it Big Mack's Little Sagebrush Ranch. Mack was a brilliant guy, no doubt about it." He then turned to Bud, "You ain't drinkin' or nuthin' are you? Why else would you need to see Indie?"

Bud grinned. "After trying to sleep on that damned couch, I could use a stiff drink, but no, I could just use some advice on how to quit fiddling. It drives Wilma Jean crazy."

He twirled the ends of his mustache, as if to demonstrate, to which Junior commented, "By the way, nice stash. I got some stash wax at the store if you need some. I had one just like it when I still had hair, and it was red like that, too. I shaved it off after I went bald cause it made my head all off kilter—the center of gravity was too low and it made me nod off all the time."

Bud grinned, then pulled off the lane and parked next to the sheriff in front of a large adobe-style house that he took to be Indie's.

"Nice place," he said, noting the extensive verandas and gardens. The huge elm trees that leaned over the house were just starting to leaf out, giving the place a sense of shelter. A small flock of bluebirds lifted from the trees as Bud and Junior got out of the FJ.

"Used to be where the original homestead stood," Junior replied. "The old Redd place. Those trees are over a hundred years old. She tore the old house down and built hers, ruined a perfectly good piece of history. Ticked everyone in the valley off."

"Why did Mack sell land to Indie? I thought he was trying to buy up the whole valley."

"He is—was, that is. He liked Indie cause she was always telling him how to live by his horoscope and get even richer than he was. She's a prosperity kind of gal, though it's all horse crap. He met her over at some whingdingdoodle in Tellyride, and they took to each other like dogs rollin' in cow manure. She's also their caretaker when they leave, feeds the horses and takes care of Maggie, their dog. So he liked that. And he wanted someone around for company for Annie, cause he was gone so much, so she wouldn't fly the coop."

"How do you know all this?"

"LuAnn. People come into the cafe and talk."

"Does Indie get along with Annie OK?"

"What? How the hell would I know something personal like that? You think I got nothing better to do than stick my nose in everybody else's business?" Junior grinned. "Far as I know, she does, but they sure don't have much in common. Annie's got her head on straight, other than being married to a jackass. She's a nice gal. Would be nice lookin', too, if she could get rid of that sadsack look she carries around all the time."

With that, they both got out of the FJ and joined Indie and Joe, who were standing by the lane, looking on down towards ranch buildings that lay maybe a quarter-mile distant.

Indie pointed at the ground and said, "See, Sheriff, there's my tracks where I walked down to the ranch this morning. And there's the tracks of the backhoe, and there's the horses' hooves. And the dog prints are Maggie's, their Australian shepherd."

"How many horses?" Joe asked.

"Three, and they're all gone. I heard them thundering off during the night, before the backhoe came through."

"Did you hear any other vehicles?" Bud asked.

"No, and they would have to come right by my house, there's no other way in. And see, there's the wire gate. Someone had to open it to let the horses out. They can't get over the cattle guard under the big log gate. And they were in a hurry, cause they didn't bother to close it."

She pointed to where the gate still lay open, the wire on the ground.

Bud watched as Junior walked over to check out the gate. He noted that Junior's pot belly was firm and round, and he wondered if his would soon look like that or would be more bouncy, though he sure wasn't adding any to it with LuAnn's cooking.

For a moment, he thought of Wilma Jean and wondered what she was doing, if she had anything special planned for lunch, maybe having her library friends over or something fun in his absence.

As if on cue, his stomach growled, and he remembered he hadn't yet had breakfast. He was setting a record for not eating, and he wondered if he might pass out soon. Oh well, if nothing else, maybe he'd lose a bit of that paunch he was working on, sitting on a tractor all day.

"See, you can tell the order everything happened," Indie was saying, "by which tracks are on top of the others." She was giving the sheriff a tracking lesson, which Bud figured he probably didn't much need.

"Looks like the horse tracks cross the road and go up on the plateau," Junior noted.

"All the saddles are still in the barn," Indie said. "And they never rode bareback."

"These aren't all horse tracks," Bud commented, looking closer.

"What are they?" asked Indie.

"Buffalo," Bud answered. "And they're on top of the horse tracks."

"Alright," Joe said. "Bud and I are going to walk over to the ranch. You two had better stay here and wait. We don't need any more prints on top of what we already have, plus who knows what we're going to find."

"Oh, no you don't," moaned Junior. "I ain't stayin' here alone."

Indie gave him a disgusted look. "Look, I'll be here with you—you won't be alone, Mr. Mayor of Nuthin'."

"Mayor?" Bud asked.

"He's the Mayor of Paradox, didn't you know that?" Indie asked. "And it's a real paradox, how he got to be mayor." She shot him a black look.

"It's not like it's some great honor," Junior said. "It's more like a prison sentence, like trying to keep order in a lunatic asylum. And she's one of the main lunatics," he added, nodding towards Indie.

Bud grinned. His uncle was Mayor of Paradox? He found that amusing, after all the complaining Junior had done all his life about government.

"Why didn't you tell me?" Bud asked.

Junior answered, "Look, Buddy, it's kind of like having a bad headache or something. You don't need to go around telling everyone about it, you just suffer in silence."

"Do you think there's been something bad happen?" Indie asked.

Joe was now starting down the lane, so Bud took off after him, leaving Junior to answer her question.

"You don't know do you?" Junior answered. "Something bad's definitely happened. Mack was murdered last night and dumped in the river with that backhoe you heard go by. Makes me wonder if Annie didn't get tired of him, kill him, take the body and the backhoe to the river, then walk back and take off on the horses with her dog. Problem is, the backhoe tracks are on top of the horse tracks. Maybe she was murdered, too, and we don't know yet where her body is."

Indie slowly sank onto a nearby garden bench, then just sat there silently, looking disoriented.

"Dammit," Junior muttered, then wandered over to look at a concrete garden statue of what looked to be a half-naked man with his hands on his big round belly, legs crossed and smiling. A robin was perched on his round bald head, but the bird wasn't concrete, it was real.

If this Buddha guy was so popular in spite of being so chubby and short and bald, maybe there was hope for himself after all, Junior mused.

He stood there, wondering if maybe he should slow down on the Oreos, as Indie finally got up and slowly walked into the house. Junior then went and sat on the bench.

He hoped Bud and Joe would get back soon, as he really needed his early afternoon cup of tea from the Paradox Cafe.

After some time, he walked over to Indie's front door and rang the doorbell, which sounded a large oriental gong.

CHAPTER 9

Not long afterwards, Bud and Sheriff Joe walked back up the lane and talked for a minute, then Joe left. Bud wasn't so sure he liked what they had talked about, which was whether or not he might be interested in hiring on to help solve the murder. He wasn't even sure he wanted to stay here one more day, given his sleeping accommodations, yet alone stay longer.

He paused, thinking he heard a train whistle, but he knew there were no trains in Paradox. He walked over to Indie's garden, where she and Junior were now sitting at a wicker table, drinking what looked to be tea from a burnt-orange porcelain teapot with matching cups.

"You guys done?" Junior asked Bud. "Indie's telling me about this way crazy people try to drive you crazy, too. It's called gas lightning."

"No, Junior, gas *lighting*, not lightning," Indie replied, exasperated.

"Yeah, and she's trying to poison me with this hoity toity stuff she calls tea, but it ain't like no tea I've ever had."

He sipped from his cup and made a face, then refilled the cup from the teapot.

Indie handed Bud a cup. "Be careful, it's hot," she said. "It's Japanese Sencha green tea with lemon, pineapple and grapefruit, called Blissful Peace. I put a little honey in it cause the way Junior acts, he needs something to sweeten him up."

Bud took the cup, holding it tentatively up to his nose, smelling the lemon. He hadn't had a cup of tea since the time he and Wilma Jean went to that new little hippie street cafe in Price, the one that didn't last long. The area's coal miners weren't much for peppermint tea and vegetarian sandwiches, Bud had guessed, though he had kind of liked it.

He and Wilma Jean had eaten lunch there after he got his ear pierced, which seemed long ago, even though it had been just a few months. He was glad that was all over, he thought, fingering where the hole in his earlobe had grown back over. He then twirled the ends of his mustache in approval.

"I wouldn't be caught dead drinking something like this," Junior said, then took another sip and screwed up his face in disgust. "At least not in public. Tastes like flowers."

"How do you know what flowers taste like?" Indie asked, then turned to Bud. "So, did you guys find anything?"

Bud nodded his head no, sipping his tea. "The sheriff is getting one of the CBI guys in to do a more thorough look, but we sure didn't find much."

"What's the CBI?" Indie asked.

"Colorado Bureau of Investigation," Bud answered. "But Indie, he wants you to stay away from there, and to call if you see anyone coming in. He doesn't want any potential evidence compromised."

"What if Annie comes back?" Indie asked.

"Call him immediately. Actually call me, at the store. At this point, she's listed as a missing person."

"I'm worried Mack did something awful to her," Indie replied.

"You have any reason to think that?" Bud asked, surprised.

"Well...maybe. She was planning on leaving him, and he wasn't too happy about it."

"Seems to me he's the one that had something awful done to him," Junior reflected. "And maybe Annie's the one who did it, then took off. Or maybe it was you—how do we know you're innocent?"

Indie looked shocked.

"I would never kill anybody! Talk about bad karma! Whatever, Junior. Maybe you did it, everyone knows you two didn't get along. But Mack really needed some internal work—he had some residual anger from some previous existence, some residue of a past life that was somehow affecting his present one. Karma, maybe..."

"Annie hated it here, didn't she?" Junior changed the subject. "I picked that up whenever she would come into the store and talk. She always wanted to go back to California."

"Well, hated is too strong of a word, maybe, but she was lonely. Mack was gone all the time playing cowboy and developer, and she was an artist, but she also liked being around people. About the only thing she liked here was going birding—Annie loves birds and this valley has lots of species. I think she was a gypsy at some point in a past incarnation. She had a freedom-loving spirit and didn't like other people telling her what to do, and Mack was always telling her what to do. She had an aura about her of wasted opportunities. She told me she was going to leave Paradox as soon as she could figure out how financially."

Indie paused to sip her tea, then added, "She felt isolated here. See, they met in Telluride, where Mack owned a big lodge. Telluride's a very electric environment with lots going on. And she was from California and missed the ocean. All in all, Paradox just wasn't her kind of place. I think they made a big mistake coming here."

"Why did they?" Bud asked.

"Annie really liked Telluride, but Mack had this scheme that, since Paradox is only a couple of hours away, he could come here and start a resort and make a lot of money, attract the well-heeled Telluride crowd. So they bought 200 acres and turned it into Big Mack's Little Ponderosa Ranch, built that nice house over there. Mack even built Annie a separate house as her art studio. He was trying to buy up the whole valley—he had grand plans, turn it into a cowboy Disneyland. But that Mack, he had a lot of imaginary things going on, wasn't grounded in reality at all. He had a negative aura. Mack wasn't even his real name."

Bud asked, "What was his real name?"

"His real name was Rudolf," Indie replied. "He changed it to Mack because he thought that was a good cowboy name. He'd been infatuated with the cowboy life ever since he was a kid. He grew up in Quebec, Canada, pretty far from cowboy country. I don't think anyone in the valley ever did really accept him, and he was aware of it. His French accent didn't help things any. He wanted to be a real cowboy, but he lacked the real cowboy kind of manner."

"Who do you think might have had a motive to murder him?" Bud asked.

"Everybody but me," Indie replied, giving Junior a dirty look. "There wasn't anyone in the valley he hadn't irritated or tried to screw over, except me, and that's only because I could see into his past and where he was coming from and outsmart him. Plus he was always telling me his plans. He had no one else to talk to. I have a set of crop-circle cards that I used on him, and it seemed to help him feel better. It affected his vibratory system. "

Bud ignored Junior's guffaw and asked, "Does he have a hired hand?"

"Yeah, Bodie Wilson. He lives across the road. Mack hired Bodie to run the farm. He does the irrigating and all that. Mack couldn't run this place without him. Bodie's an Aquarius and I can sometimes see a pale aura around him, and I think he's going through some kind of personal transformation. But Bodie's too nice to kill Mack, though he probably isn't mourning him much."

"And who's the neighbor over across the way?" Bud asked, nodding towards a huge log house that sat a quarter-mile or so down the main road.

"That's Tom and Susie Turner. They moved here from Arkansas, bought the ranch next door and built a mansion. They're very wealthy—they have a chain of restaurants. Tom's a railroad buff like Junior here, sort of a regressed personality. He hated Mack. Some kind of male rivalry thing. I think they both have a lot of inner work needing done."

"Had, in Mack's case," Junior commented wryly. "And at least trains are real, unlike crop circles, which are total cow manure."

Bud stood, hoping to avert an argument, setting his cup on the table. "Well, Indie, you've been a great source of information, but we need to get back. I need to get some breakfast. I got sidetracked talking to my wife earlier and never did eat."

"You're married?" Indie asked.

Junior grinned. "Yeah, he's spoken for, Indie, so don't get no ideas."

"You know, Junior, I'm going to tell you something important, so listen very carefully," Indie said slowly, irritated. "Your aura has been especially reddish lately, which is the color of passion. I don't know what you're up to, but be careful. And I've noticed LuAnn's is the same color these days."

Junior's face now matched his supposed aura.

Indie added, "And Bud, yours is blue, which means honesty and integrity, but I'm noticing it's not quite as bright as it should be, which means possible ill health."

Junior snorted. "Yeah, ill health alright, he's half sick from drinking lemon, pineapple, and grapefruit tea."

"If anything, I think it's sleep-deprivation," said Bud. "But thanks for everything, Indie, and stay in touch if you see anything out of the norm."

Junior replied, "Don't say that, Bud, she'll be calling you ten times a day. She's always seeing things out of the norm."

Indie gave Junior another dirty look, but he just grinned back.

"Thanks, Indie. Keep us posted," Bud said. As he walked to the gate, he noted a short wooden spear mounted on the wall of the veranda. "Wow, that could be lethal. It looks African."

Indie paused, then replied guardedly, "It is. My mentor said I needed to go to Africa if I wanted to progress spiritually, so I did. It was the journey of a lifetime. I was given the spear by the leader of the Hottentot Tribe. He told me I was a gifted seeker and highly evolved, but that I needed to free myself from rules. The spear was symbolic of cutting free from everything."

"Why keep something so unique out here in the weather?" Bud asked, gingerly fingering the sharp tip.

"Because I'm a pacifist and don't like things with potential for violence in the house, symbolic or not," Indie replied.

"Musta been a little guy," Junior remarked. "That's a pretty short spear."

Indie shrugged. "Yes, he was small."

"With something that sharp, all you need is a good aim," Bud observed. "Size doesn't matter."

"True," Indie replied. "And they use poison on the tip."

Bud grimaced and pulled his hand back, rubbing it on his pants.

"Better not eat any finger foods, Buddy my boy, unless you wash your hands first," Junior grinned. "Let's git!"

With that, Bud and Junior got into the FJ and drove under the sign that read "Big Mack's Little Ponderosa Ranch" and headed back down the road.

CHAPTER 10

Bud had eaten a hamburger from the Paradox Cafe and was now resting on the cot he'd set up in Junior's living room, his lack of sleep finally catching up with him.

As he lay there, he could hear Junior downstairs in the store greeting people, the screen door slamming as customers came and went.

Bud couldn't figure out the events of the past 24 hours, and it was bothering him. No one else seemed to see the inconsistency of Mack Murphy being murdered for doing what developers do, buying and developing land. Even when people didn't like development, they typically didn't murder the guy doing the job, even if they disliked him. And apparently Mack had threatened Junior and who knows who else for not selling to him, but still, that was no reason to murder the guy.

Mack was disliked, that was pretty much a given at this point, at least by Junior and LuAnn. But what had happened to his wife Annie, and who was the person with the limp driving the backhoe? And where were the horses and the dog, Maggie? And why had the wild man conked Uncle Junior on the head and then gone fishing the next morning at the river instead of heading back up onto the Uncompahgre Plateau, where he belonged?

Bud sighed and stretched out. He hadn't felt this fatigued for a long time, and he was wishing he was back home. He missed Wilma Jean and the dogs, even though he'd only been gone a little over a day. It seemed longer, and he had a suspicion things here were just getting going. And to make things worse, he was going to miss his favorite TV show this evening, Scooby Doo.

He knew he didn't have to stay, and he toyed with the idea of taking a nap, then heading on back home in the evening. He could be there in a couple of hours and surprise Wilma Jean by showing up at the leagues. He used to bowl some—that's where he'd met her, at her bowling alley there in Radium, Sink Hole Lanes.

He could hear a woodpecker tapping on the wall outside, and the rhythm soon lulled him into nodding off, just as the phone rang, waking him with a start. It was an extension to the one downstairs in the store, so Bud ignored it, knowing Junior would answer.

But nobody answered, and it continued to ring, so Bud finally jumped up and grabbed the old turquoise phone off the wall. But before he could say "Yell-ow," he could hear someone already talking. Apparently Junior had picked up after all. Bud started to hang up, but then he heard his name and couldn't help but listen.

"Junior speaking."

"Junior, what the hell's going on around here?"

"Buddy's here, and he's going to figure it all out," Junior said.

"You mean your lawman nephew over there in Utah? He's here? What the hell's he doing here? This is nobody's business but us here in the valley."

Bud didn't recognize the voice, and it sounded irritated.

Junior replied, "It's his business now because I say it is, and I'm the mayor."

The voice replied, "Well, Mister Mayor, you better tell your nephew to watch his step because there's more going on here than meets the eye. Sure would hate to see him get hurt—or worse, end up like Mack."

Junior's voice sounded tense. "What do you know about Mack?"

Now the voice sounded placating. "Junior, I don't know anything about what happened to Mack, that's why I called you, but the fact they found his body in the river this morning is all over the valley. I just don't want to see nobody else hurt, and your nephew has no idea what kind of hornet's nest he just stepped into."

"That hornet's nest should be pretty much gone, now that Mack's dead."

"Don't kid yourself, Junior. I think Paradox is about to have a big gold rush. Then there will be hornet's nests all over the place."

With that, the caller hung up. Bud could hear Junior still breathing on the phone, so he asked, "Who was that, Uncle?"

Junior sounded surprised. "You heard all that?"

"Yeah, but accidentally."

"Good. I'm glad you heard that, because now I have a witness. That was Turner—we're supposed to be friends. He's Mack's neighbor, and he knows something I sure as hell don't know, but I aim to find out."

Bud replied, "Don't you mean that you aim for me to find out?"

"Isn't that what I said?" Junior asked. "I'll be right up."

"Bring that stash wax up with you."

Junior was soon up the stairs, and he handed Bud a small tin that said, "Captain Twain's Mustache Wax." Bud opened it and put a little on the ends of his mustache, then twirled them a bit.

"Looks good," Junior commented. "Makes the ends stick out all pointy. Just what you needed. You must get that red hair from us O'Connor's side of the family."

"Must be," Bud replied, not wanting to mention that his lawman grandfather on his dad's side also had red hair. No point in bringing up old family stuff.

"Or maybe from your grandpa on your daddy's side," Junior said, grinning. "Anyway, Buddy, I know you're all tired out, but are you wanting to stay and help out with all this or go home? Now, that's what they call a rhetorical question, and I know you wanna go home, but maybe you could stay a couple more days until things settle down. I'm pretty worried about that wild man, myself. Somebody who knows what he's doing needs to figure all this out, and that would be you, assuming your sickly aura can handle it."

Junior grinned, then continued. "And you can have my bed tonight. I sleep on the couch half the time, anyway. Let's go get some dinner over at LuAnn's. I'll buy, as long as you stay away from the righthand side of the menu, where the expensive stuff is."

"I just ate not too long ago," Bud replied.

"That's OK, it won't hurt you to eat again, you're a growing boy," Junior answered, poking Bud where his stomach hung a little over his belt buckle.

Bud grimaced and followed his uncle down the stairs and out the door.

CHAPTER 11

Bud gently touched the sides of his horse with his boot heels, urging her on up the steep trail. Sheriff Joe had called Bud earlier asking if he'd ride with him onto the plateau to see if they could find any trace of Annie, but he'd been called away on an emergency at the last minute, leaving Bud to go it solo.

Joe had provided the horse, a pretty black on white Paint, who he'd said was called "Weezee." Bud hadn't had time to ask if she was called that as a nickname for Louise or because she wheezed when being ridden.

Right now, as they climbed up and up, Weezee was beginning to wheeze, but Bud figured he would, too, if he were carrying some guy who'd eaten two dinners the night before.

Uncle Junior had offered to go along, but then decided at the last minute that his horsemanship (or lack thereof) would just slow everyone down, since he'd never ridden a horse.

Bud had agreed, as the trail up through the cliffs looked to be nerve wracking for even a seasoned rider. In fact, Bud was at this moment contemplating getting off and letting Weezee lead while he held onto her tail to pull him up.

It was a technique he'd used many times when he was a kid on the Preston Nutter Ranch over in Nine Mile Canyon in Utah, where his grandpa had been a cowboy before going into law enforcement. Bud had spent the summers out there when he was a teenager, helping out and earning a little spending money. His grandpa had taught him the fine art of riding, and Bud was now glad for it, even though it had been awhile since he'd been on horseback.

Weezee must be in pretty good shape, Bud thought, as she deftly followed the trail from Mack's ranch, cutting through a cleft in the band of sheer Wingate cliffs that surrounded the Paradox Valley. It was the only way up onto the plateau without driving up out of the valley and backtracking on old timber roads.

He'd gotten a late start, nearly noon, as it had taken awhile for Joe to bring the horse. Bud figured he'd go as far as he could, then resume the search in earnest tomorrow.

Today would be a recon sort of day, let him get used to the lay of the land. Maybe Joe would be able to accompany him later for a more thorough search.

They soon topped out and Bud pulled back on the reins, letting Weezee catch her breath while he surveyed the valley below. It was now obvious why the rift was called the Paradox Valley—the Dolores River cut through the valley at a 90-degree angle to the way the valley ran, not at all what one would expect—a paradox.

The valley wasn't carved by the river at all, but was the result of an underlying collapsed salt dome, just like the valley over in his hometown of Radium across the flanks of the Salt Mountains. In fact, it was technically the same valley and the Salts had pushed up through it, and the Paradox Valley now sat on the opposite side from Radium.

Bud sat and studied the Salts, unfamiliar with this view of their backsides. They looked like an entirely different mountain range, yet had a familiar feel. He watched as a flock of pinion jays circled overhead with their incessant chattering, then flew on over the rim.

Finally, when Weezee began to breathe normally, Bud turned her and headed on up the Uncompahgre Plateau. He could see its flanks gradually rising above to a deceptively high flattop of almost 10,000 feet. The plateau just didn't look that high from below, much to the chagrin of a number of pilots who had failed to negotiate enough altitude and ended up crashed in the thick aspen and spruce forests that blanketed the area.

It was a wild place, stretching from Pinon Mesa in Utah clear over to the edge of the San Juan Mountains in Colorado. Its lower flanks were covered with sagebrush and scrub oak and crisscrossed with old logging and access roads for ranchers who ran cattle and sheep there. Higher up, it was cloaked with ponderosa pine, aspen, spruce, and fir forests, home to numerous black bears—and also to the wild man.

The plateau had seen its share of range wars at the end of the 1800s, with a kind of truce finally being made between the cattlemen and the sheepmen—the cattlemen ran their stock on the northern end of the plateau, and the Basque and Mexican sheepherders claimed the southern end, where they carved their names and art into the aspen bark. The Paradox Valley was more towards the northern end of the plateau and was thus cattle country.

Joe had told Bud of a few line camps he might want to check if he had time, places where Annie could potentially hide, as they were usually stocked with food for cowboys checking on the cattle. She could even keep the horses up there, as the camps had corrals and were usually by one of the many small streams that drained the area.

The climb was now gradual, the trail winding through thick stands of scrub oak. At one point, Weezee startled a small flock of wild turkeys, but she didn't even blink an eye, even though the large birds made lots of noise flapping their wings. Bud was thankful he'd been given a trail-wise horse. He wanted to focus on the search, not on staying on board.

Once on top, Bud was now enjoying the ride, recalling all the good times he'd had as a kid on horseback, all the places he'd explored. He began daydreaming about he and Wilma Jean getting a couple of horses—they had room on their two acres, even an old barn.

He wondered if Hoppie and Pierre could keep up, then decided it probably wouldn't be a good idea to take them along. Maybe he could fix up some kind of backpacks for them.

The trail now became steep again as it wound up through a small rock outcropping. A canyon wren called out, its descending crescendo reminding Bud of good times he'd spent in the canyon country of Utah. Wild rose grew everywhere, and the tiny pink flowers were beginning to bud out, giving the place the look of an English country garden.

As they switchbacked further up the rocks, Bud spied a small spring, its water running along the trail in a shallow stream. He stopped and let Weezee have her head and drink. As he was noting the water had a reddish tint, probably from iron, he saw horses' hoofprints on the trail, which then veered off, heading down a small ravine to the right. If he hadn't stopped to water Weezee, he would never have seen them, he mused, and would've just kept riding.

Standing up in his stirrups, he tried to see down the ravine through the thick brush, wondering if this was where Joe had said one of the line camps was located. Line camps are always on roads or trails, where they can be resupplied, and there was neither down there, just more thick scrub oak with what appeared to be a rough animal trail cutting through it. But it was possible a road came in from below, he thought.

The small stream followed the ravine and could possibly feed a stock pond below, which could be a good place for a line camp, but Bud's instincts told him something wasn't right.

He paused, then turned Weezee and headed down the ravine, following what was left of the horses' hoofprints, aware of every rock and every tree that could serve as an ambush. Weezee balked, but he kept after her, kicking her lightly with his heels. He had the uncontrollable urge to twirl the ends of his mustache, but needed to hang onto the reins so she wouldn't turn around.

Weezee again balked, but Bud pressed on, even though for some reason, his enjoyable ride had just turned into one with that heightened awareness that says your life could be in danger.

CHAPTER 12

It was slow going through the thick bushes, even with the narrow animal trail to follow. Branches whipped back, whacking Bud in the face and nearly sweeping him out of the saddle more than once. He watched for ticks, as this was prime tick territory, but he didn't see any. Maybe it was still too cold up here, he thought.

Finally, after a somewhat torturous ride, the ravine opened up and the trail cut through a large meadow filled with grasses, skunkbush, and horsetails where the stream widened out. A purple martin sat in the aspens, eyeing them but unafraid.

Bud stopped and got off Weezee, letting her graze a bit, as she seemed to have settled down. He ate the PBJ sandwich he'd made earlier and drank a root beer from his pack.

Bud noted a large bank of loose dirt to the far side of the meadow and thought he saw movement. He threw a bit of his sandwich over there, and sure enough, a large marmot came out of a hole and grabbed it, sitting on its hind legs while munching away. For some reason, it kind of reminded him of Uncle Junior, though he would never tell his uncle that. He wished Junior had come along, even if he hadn't ever ridden before.

For some reason, Bud felt unsettled and on edge. He usually enjoyed solitude and being alone in wild places, but today he was wishing for company. Maybe it was the knowledge that he was in wild man territory, and he still hadn't forgotten the size and ominous feeling he'd had when watching whatever it was running from the back of Junior's store. He hoped he wouldn't run into it, especially alone here in its own backyard.

He then thought about Annie and her old dog, Maggie. Had Annie fled up here? It would make sense, if she'd been in a hurry, to just jump on one of the horses and take off, leaving the gate open, the others and Maggie following. Had she come up into this wild place as a refuge? Surely she knew about the wild man and that this was his home. Was she afraid of him? Was she still alive, or had he killed her by now?

He pulled Weezee's head up from the grass and put his foot in the stirrup, swinging his other leg over her back and settling into the saddle. He felt safer on the horse, as she could make good time if she needed to, taking him back down to the valley.

Weezee started off at a fast walk, but Bud pulled her up, stopping. Why was he feeling so nervous he wondered. He watched Weezee's ears to see if she was feeling the same way, but she seemed relaxed. Must be his imagination, he figured, starting her on the trail again. He really wished he were here under different circumstances so he could enjoy the ride.

The meadow stretched out for quite a ways, and the going was now easy. The three horses' hoofprints were now more obvious in the soft dirt.

But now Bud saw something he didn't like, something he'd seen yesterday in the mud down by the river—there, right in the trail, were the same huge footprints, barefoot prints that looked like a large human's. Bud pulled Weezee up and stopped, feeling a chill. He was definitely in the wild man's territory, and he didn't like that one bit.

He thought about turning back. The sun was getting lower, and he figured it was about three p.m., but it was still early enough in the season that the sun was down by about six. He'd been riding for a few hours, but it didn't seem like it. If he turned around now, he'd get out about dark, and he didn't want to negotiate that steep stretch down off the rim with no light to see by.

But something made him keep going. He decided to ride to the end of the meadow and see where the trail went, then turn back. It looked like only another half-mile or so and shouldn't take long, and he was thinking he maybe could see something there in the trees. There might be a line camp down there, he thought.

As he got closer to the edge of the forest where the meadow ended, he began to feel that unsettled feeling even stronger, the one he'd learned not to ignore when he was working in law enforcement. He took his Ruger from its shoulder holster and put it in his jacket pocket, where he could keep his hand on it, safety still on. He pulled Weezee to a stop again and watched her, but she seemed relaxed, so he continued.

The shadows were now lengthening, and he was near the forest's edge, the trees casting long dark ominous shadows. There was no sign of a line camp, but something was different—he couldn't quite put his finger on it, but it made him wish he were back home in his little bungalow in Green River. He wanted badly to turn back, but his analytic side wanted an answer.

He was now directly under the trees at the edge of the forest, big yellow-bellied ponderosas that made him think of Big Mack's Little Ponderosa Ranch, except these were big, tall, old-growth trees, not little at all.

Bud loved ponderosas—they usually grew in big meadows with very little understory, making one feel like they were in a big natural park, and he loved the vanilla smell of the bark. He leaned back, looking up into the trees. He didn't think he'd ever seen ponderosas this large.

But now he thought he could see something up in the tree, and it didn't look natural. And there, in that tree over there, was another. And another over there! The trees looked like they had platforms in them, and on each platform he could make something out, something kind of yellowish-white.

He rode over directly under one and looked up—sure enough, a platform, made of various large limbs. His curiosity getting the better of him, Bud got off Weezee and tied her to a small tree, then looked up into one of the big trees. He wanted to get up high enough to see what was on the platforms.

He began climbing, not an easy task because of the many small limbs that poked him, but he managed to get up far enough that he could see onto a platform over on the next tree. And what he saw made him shiver, quickly shimmy back down the tree, untie Weezee, and decide it was time to leave.

Each platform held a skeleton, very old and sun bleached. They lay there as they had for maybe centuries, arms crossed, pieces of tanned deer hide still hanging off them, clothing long decayed. He was in some kind of grave-yard, but an open-air one. His feeling about the big ponde-rosas had now turned to one of horror.

But as he started to get on Weezee, he noticed some-thing in the dirt, something shiny. He bent down and picked it up—it was a nail, one not all that old, and next to it was a piece of something yellowish-white. Puzzled, he examined it. It was a small chunk of plastic.

As he got onto the horse and turned her to head back down the trail, he heard a scream from the trees that made his blood run cold. It wasn't far away, and it echoed through the forest like a freight train. Whatever was mak-ing it had huge lungs and sounded angry.

Bud started to kick Weezee into a run, but it wasn't nec-essary, as her back hocks were already well under her as she lunged forward like a bronc leaving a rodeo chute.

And just then, coming up behind him, Bud heard the sound of pounding hooves. He turned just enough to see three horses, all in a dead run straight for him. Before he could even process what was happening, they had overtak-en him and Weezee, and he was now part of the thunder-ing herd as Weezee ran away with him. It was all he could do to hang on tight and hope he wasn't knocked off by a tree limb or scrub-oak branch.

He hoped he could get control of the horse before they came to the steep trail that wound down through the cliffs. If not, he knew he was a goner.

CHAPTER 13

Weezee was not going to stop, no matter what Bud did. He tried pulling back as hard as he could on the reins, but it felt like she'd somehow managed to get the bit between her teeth, and his pulling had no effect.

He tried shortening one rein and forcing her head to turn, which was a surefire way to stop a runaway, but she just kept going, head turned half towards him, until he quickly eased up, fearing she would fall.

She was terrified, and having the other horses running beside her just added to the panic. Bud finally gave up and just held on, as the horses followed the trail back to the valley.

When they finally got to the rim, Weezee paused just long enough for Bud to kick his feet out of the stirrups and bail, tumbling into the soft sand, right before she took off where the trail wound down through the rimrock.

There was no way he could stay on her if she tried to run down that steep slope, and it was quite possible he would throw her off balance and they would both fall to the valley floor. Better to risk a broken bone by bailing now than certain death.

Bud rolled a couple of times, then lay there for a minute, gathering himself, checking to see if he was OK. So far so good, but he knew he was going to be sore where he'd hit the sand with his left side. He was glad his Ruger was in his other pocket.

He slowly stood, then slipped behind a large rock near the trail, as he wasn't so sure the wild man or whatever had made that scream wasn't following, and he wanted to be as cautious as possible. Something had terrified the horses, something that he had no desire to meet up with.

He stayed behind the rock, well hidden. It would soon be dark, and he needed to get going in order to navigate the steep trail. It would be too tricky trying to hike down it in the dark. But something told him to stay put for a bit and assess the situation.

Sure enough, not long after, he could see something coming along the trail in the deepening shadows. It was hard to make out what it was, but he could tell it walked on two legs.

As he held his breath, he could see that the figure was definitely not as large as the wild man and walked with a slight limp, and whoever it was, they were in a hurry.

They were quickly next to him, and in the darkening shadows he caught a glimpse of blonde hair under a base-ball cap and tucked down into the collar of a ranch jacket. It was a woman, and he guessed this to be Annie, but couldn't be sure, having never actually met her. All he'd seen was the photo of her and Mack's wedding that sat on their fireplace mantle.

She was soon gone, down the trail over the rim, with no hesitation. Bud wanted to follow, but his instincts said to stay hidden. Sure enough, another figure soon came down the trail, this one much larger.

Bud cringed, knowing it was the wild man, hoping it wouldn't be able to smell or sense his presence. Bud ducked further down behind the rock as the large figure came loping by, then cautiously peeked out as it continued on. Sure enough, it was going on down the trail, following the horses. It was large and black, and Bud was sure it's what had made the scream, yet something was different about it, as it wasn't quite the same as when he'd seen it at Junior's store. It seemed bigger.

Bud sat for a moment after it disappeared down the trail, wondering what to do. He wasn't prepared to spend the night up here, and yet he didn't want to follow it down—it could turn back and meet him.

As he sat there, he could feel the soreness already setting in along his left side where he'd bit the dust, and he knew if he didn't start moving soon, he'd be too stiff to negotiate the steep trail ahead.

He stood, stretching out the sore leg and arm on his left side, then decided to go look over the edge and see if he could make anything out. Standing there, he could see a dust cloud partway down the trail, and he knew the horses were still making good time, but he couldn't make out the woman or the wild man, as it was too dark.

He stood there and watched for a moment, trying to decide whether to continue on down now or wait a bit. As he stood watching, he suddenly felt something brush against the back of his leg. He about jumped out of his skin, quickly turning around, gun drawn like lightning.

There, in the shadows, stood a dog, a white and tan Australian Shepherd, wagging its tail and looking very tired and hungry, its long thick hair matted and dirty. It must be Maggie!

Bud slowly held his hand out, talking gently, saying "Maggie" over and over, and the dog came up and let him pet her. He could tell she was worn out. He wasn't sure what was going on, but to find the horses and also Maggie made Bud sure that Annie must be the figure with the blonde hair.

At this point, Bud decided he would try his luck and go on down the trail. If he met the wild man, at least he was armed, though he suspected his Ruger wouldn't make much of a dent in the large creature. He called Maggie to follow as he started off the rim, but she just stood and watched him.

No way was he going to leave Maggie here, so Bud took off his belt and made a leash, looping it around her collar, then called her again and stepped forward, gently pulling. But Maggie wouldn't budge. She turned and started back up the trail in the direction they'd just come, as if trying to get Bud to follow her.

Bud was torn. He knew Maggie was trying to lead him somewhere. Maybe Maggie wasn't aware that Annie had gone on down the trail, and Maggie was trying to get help. Bud wondered if Hoppie or Pierre would do the same for him—maybe, he thought, if he had a package of hot dogs or something good to eat.

It was almost dark, and he needed to get back down into the valley. Weezee had taken his food and water in the saddlebags, and he didn't even have a jacket with him, as that had been tied to the cantle of the saddle. It was still spring, and he knew it would get cold at night. He had no flashlight and no matches, things he always carried in his jacket pocket.

Finally, as Maggie pulled on him again, he turned and followed. He didn't want to go down that rim trail with the wild man ahead of him anyway. At least he knew the wild man was down there and not up here.

If he got lost, well, so be it, he would surely survive a night out and could go home in the morning. But he had to take the chance and see what Maggie was trying to show him. He really had no other choice.

He followed as the old dog led him back up the trail, her drooping tail slowly wagging.

CHAPTER 14

Bud was having trouble hanging onto Maggie, as her night vision seemed much better than his. For an old dog, she sure could pull, he thought, wondering where they were going to end up.

They'd been walking for at least an hour, and a couple of times he'd caught his toe on a root or rock and almost fallen. He wasn't sure if he could survive another fall, as his left side was now really sore, and he was beginning to think the old dog was lost.

It was hard holding onto the belt he'd rigged up as a leash, as it was slick leather, but before long, Maggie finally stopped. By now it was pretty much dark, but he could make out some kind of structure, although he wasn't sure what it could be.

It seemed it was actually a post of some kind, and Maggie again began pulling, this time in a more circular fashion. She rounded the post and continued at a right angle until they came to another post. Bud was puzzled. The posts were large and leaned a bit inward.

But now Maggie pulled upward, and Bud realized they were at a set of stairs. What the heck, he wondered, stairs out in the middle of a forest? He dutifully followed, though it was hard to see, but he knew they were now going up.

Up and up they went—Bud was now thinking they were climbing a tower of some kind. Sure enough, they finally came to what appeared to be a deck, and then a door.

Maggie scratched on the door as if she were home and wanted in, but no one answered. Bud wished again he had a flashlight, but at least he now knew where they were— they were at the old Ute Lookout Tower, high on the flanks of the plateau. He'd never actually been to it before, but he knew it was the only one up here and had been abandoned for a long time. The advent of satellite technology had rendered most fire lookout towers obsolete.

He slowly turned the door knob, and they went in. Bud felt around the room a bit, and sure enough, he finally found a flashlight. It was actually more of a spotlight, and it lit up the entire room when he turned it on.

Maggie was over in the corner of the room drinking from a water dish. She obviously knew where she was. Bud surveyed the room—it had a camp cot, a couple of folding camp chairs, and a large wooden work table built against one wall. Bud knew this was where the fire lookouts had kept their equipment, which probably had included a radio and an Osborne Fire Finder, a device used to triangulate locations so one could describe where the fire was.

The room was totally bare, except the bed, where a sleeping bag and a woman's sweater lay neatly folded.

Somehow, this had to be where Annie was staying, Bud thought, but why was an old dog like Maggie out wandering the forest alone?

Bud walked over to the table, where he'd noticed what looked like a small notebook. He opened it, and the first words he read were, "How could I possibly kill my own husband?"

The writing was small and hard to read, and he quickly thumbed through the rest of the notebook, but that one sentence was all it held. His right hand was twirling his mustache, but he wasn't even aware of it.

Maggie had now jumped up onto the bed, as if it were a familiar place. She looked at Bud with a sad look that he interpreted to mean something like, "Where's my mom?"

He went over and sat beside her, patting her head. He turned off the spotlight, as he didn't want anyone to know he was here—but he was too late, from the sound he could now hear below the tower, a low growling that seemed to resonate like a distant freight train, but at a lower volume.

Maggie's ears went back. As the growl beneath them ramped up in volume, she whined and began shivering, then jumped off the bed and hid under the big work table.

Bud pulled out his Ruger and took off the safety, but he knew deep inside his gun was no match for what was below them. This was no bear nor mountain lion that one could possibly scare off with a few gunshots. And actually shooting it was beyond the question, as there was no way his gun would make a dent.

As he sat there in the darkness, the growling stopped, but now something was shaking the tower! Bud couldn't believe it, the strength this thing had was tremendous. It must be pushing one of the supports back and forth. Bud wondered if it would shear off. He could picture the tower collapsing with him and Maggie in it, as it wasn't a very solid structure, just basically a small cabin on stilts.

Suddenly, the thing below started screaming. Bud's blood ran cold. He knew then it was definitely the same creature he'd heard over in the trees that had scared the horses. The thing was right beneath him, and the sound reverberated and made his ears ring, it was so loud. Apparently it had come back up the rim trail and followed him.

Bud then suddenly realized that the ringing was his cell phone. He couldn't believe it—there must be service up here on the plateau. He was amazed, then remembered there was a cell tower on the Salt Mountains, not all that far away. It wasn't accessible from the Paradox Valley, but up here was another matter.

Bud looked at his caller ID—it was Howie! Leave it to Howie to call at the most inopportune time imaginable—or maybe it was the best time, as Bud could at least tell him where he was and what was going on. Howie could call Wilma Jean and tell her he was about to be killed by what appeared to be a wild man. The miracles of modern technology, he thought wryly.

"Yell-ow," he answered in a whisper.

"Is that you, Sheriff? I can barely hear you."

"It's me, Howie. What's up?"

"Oh man, Sheriff, I just had to call you. For some reason you're not coming through very loud."

"Sorry about that, Howie, I can't talk very loud right now. What's up?"

"I probably shouldn't be calling you, as it's getting kind of late, but I just wanted to share something with you."

Bud sighed. Good old Howie. Getting information from him was like trying to spread cold honey on a peanut-butter sandwich.

"Go ahead, Howie, but I can't talk long."

"Oh man, I was riding around in the patrol vehicle, and I got out by Krider's Farm, you know, where you work when you work, and this song just popped into my head. You gotta hear it."

"How's Professor Krider, Howie? Have you seen him around at all?" Bud suddenly missed his employer and being on the farm. He wished he were home, partly because he missed his wife and the dogs, and partly because he could hear the deep growling again, and it sounded now like it was coming up the stairs.

"I dunno, Sheriff, I haven't seen him around. Someone said he was in Texas visiting relatives. But hey, wanna hear the song I made up?"

"Sure, Howie, but you'll have to make it quick. After this, would you call Wilma Jean for me and tell her I'm OK, I just can't call her right now? Tell her I'm up at the Ute Tower on the plateau and to call Junior and tell him."

"Sure, I'll do that, but you really should check in once in awhile—you know we're all kind of wondering what you're doing over there. And don't forget to put in a good word for us if there's a place we could play in Paradox."

"I'll do that, Howie."

Bud could now hear something walking along the deck outside, something big, making the boards creak. He crawled over and joined Maggie where she lay shivering under the work table.

"The song's called 'Wild Thing,' Sheriff. I know there was a hit song called that back some years ago, but this is different. It's a country-swing song. It starts out, 'Wild thing,' and then I yodel a bit, and then sing:
You're the wild thing in my heart, darlin',
I loved you from the start, darlin',
But then you started snarlin', darlin',
And my life's all torn apart, darlin,'

"And then I yodel some more and play a riff on my new guitar while Maureen plays some honky tonk piano. I don't quite have the riff down yet, but I'm workin' on it. Whattya think, Sheriff?"

Now the thing was at the door, trying to get in, shaking it. Bud sat under the table with his Ruger pointed square at where it would enter. He was terrified, but managed to answer Howie, "It's great, Howie, but I gotta go, there's someone at the door. Don't forget to call my wife."

"Whoever it is, tell them the Ramblin' Road Rangers are gonna be a big hit someday and to come to our concerts. If they're a friend of yours, we'll let them in free, since you're our manager. OK, 10-4 and over."

With that, Howie hung up, just as the beast tore the doorknob off and pushed opened the door, slamming it against the interior wall.

CHAPTER 15

Bud cringed and tried to make himself smaller up against the wall under the work table, holding Maggie close. He was tempted to use the spotlight, shining it in the wild man's eyes and blinding him, but he knew it would also reveal his hiding place.

But as soon as the door slammed against the wall, he heard another door slam, but this one under the tower. It sounded like a vehicle door.

Even though it was pitch dark, he could sense the wild man had also heard it and paused. Now the sound of people talking drifted up the steps and through the open door, and suddenly, the wild man turned and fled. It sounded to Bud like it had shimmied down one of the posts opposite where the car had parked. Bud was relieved, to say the least.

Now Maggie had come out from under the table and was wagging her tail. Bud could hear a woman's voice talking, as well as a man's. He knew Annie had to be outside.

Maggie bounded towards the door, dragging Bud's belt, which was still tied to her collar. Bud instantly wished he'd retrieved it, but he had no idea Annie would be back.

For a second, he toyed with the idea of shimmying down the post like the wild man had, but no way was he going to be out there in the blackness alone, or worse, with the wild man. He'd rather take his chances in here with Annie and whoever was with her.

Now he could hear someone climb the tower steps and then come in the open door, waving a small flashlight around.

"Dang, I know I didn't leave this door open," the woman's voice said with concern.

"Maybe the wind blew it open," a voice answered, a voice Bud had heard before but wasn't quite able to recognize.

"Oh my God! It's Maggie! Maggie, where in the world did you go? I've been so worried about you!"

"What happened?" asked a different man's voice, one Bud also knew he should recognize but didn't.

"I was in such a hurry to get out of here—I could hear the wild man screaming in the distance, and suddenly the horses all took off running. They just broke through the fence—they were terrified. I took off, too, and Maggie was right behind me. Then she just disappeared. I had to go on down without her, as the wild man wasn't far behind me. I hoped and prayed she would be alright. Oh, Maggie, what a scare you've given me!"

"What's that thing dragging after her?" one of the men asked.

"I don't know," Annie paused, then added, "Well, that's weird. It looks like someone tied a belt to her collar. Maybe someone found her, that's why she didn't follow me. She must've broken free and come back here. But it sure would be strange for someone to be up here in the dark. Especially with that wild man around."

Annie paused again, thinking, then added, "Anyway, let me grab my things, then let's get out of here. I have no idea where the wild man is, and I don't want to find out. I really appreciate you guys helping me out like this."

"It's OK, Mrs. Murphy. We're really sorry to hear about your husband, and we want you to know we're doing everything we can to help find whoever killed him."

Now the second voice added, "Yeah, we're working with that private investigator. We'll find the killer, Mrs. Murphy, you can be sure of that."

Bud now recognized the voices. It was Jimmy and Carl, the young guys he'd met down at the river.

Annie gasped. "A private investigator?"

"Yeah, his name is Bud Shumway, and he's been hired by the mayor to come in and figure it all out. From what we heard, he's the man to do it, too. He was real nice to us, and now we're helping him out."

Bud almost groaned out loud. This was news to him, and so much for being anonymous.

"You mean Mayor Junior?" Annie asked. "Oh, Lord."

Annie was scanning the flashlight around the room, making sure she had everything, and Bud just knew they would see him, but fortunately they didn't, even though Maggie came back under the table for a minute, wagging her tail.

Bud did manage to see a bit of Annie in the backlight, though not well enough that he would ever recognize her on the street. But he could tell that she was tall and had blonde hair, and as she turned and walked across the room, he noticed she had a slight limp.

Now the voices trailed off as the trio started down the stairs, Maggie following close behind. For a moment, Bud considered going with them. The thought of being alone up here in the dark was a bit unsettling.

He crawled out from under the table, then stood and looked out the open door, watching as the flashlight wobbled its way down the stairs. He heard the vehicle doors slam and the engine start and slowly fade as they drove back down the road.

Bud thought about his belt and groaned. He wouldn't miss it much, as he was needing it less and less with each of Wilma Jean's good home-cooked meals, but he had a special place in his heart for that belt buckle.

He'd earned it on the leagues back when they lived in Radium, back when he'd first met Wilma Jean at her bowling alley. It was his favorite buckle, even more so than the one he'd won riding the mechanical bull up at the Bull Riders in the Sky contest at the Big Bull Corral in Price when he was younger.

It was irreplaceable. It read, "Winning Team, Midnight Bowl." He shook his head, doubting if he would ever see it again.

But his concerns were soon forgotten as he heard the vehicle coming back up the steep hill as if they'd forgotten something. He dived back under the table.

CHAPTER 16

Bud heard the vehicle pull up under the tower, then two vehicle doors slammed. He could now hear footsteps coming up the stairs, just like before, and could make out a flashlight beam shining on the deck. He wondered why they'd come back.

The door still stood open, almost torn off its hinges where the wild man had slammed it open, and soon Bud saw a head backlit against the night sky. It was kind of a shiny head, he noted, so shiny it almost reflected the brighter stars.

Just then, he heard a voice calling out, somewhat tentatively, "Buddy, you in here?"

A second voice, though this one a bit higher, repeated the question. "Bud, you here?"

It was Junior and Indie!

Bud scooted out from under the table and answered, "Right here."

Junior jumped, startled, and aimed the flashlight directly at Bud's eyes, then asked, "What the heck you doing up here, hiding under that table? Ain't you got any sense, Nephew? A sensible man would be down at LuAnn's hash house having some bossy in a bowl and a cuppa mud, not hanging out up here with the hoot owls."

"What's that?" asked Indie.

"Hoot owl? It's a bird," Junior replied.

Indie sounded exasperated. "No, the 'bossy in a bowl' stuff."

"It's hobo for beef stew," Junior said. "Now, Bud, if you wanna get yourself up, we'll get on outta here muy pronto. This place doesn't have that sense of stability I like. Too damn rickety."

Bud stood, brushing himself off. He scanned the table top, but the notebook was gone. Annie must've taken it, he thought.

Junior seemed to be in a hurry to leave, and Bud had no objections to that, so the three of them were soon down off the tower and in Junior's old pickup, Indie making Bud ride in the middle, as she refused to sit next to Junior.

"You happen to have any water or anything?" Bud asked. He was thirsty, not having had anything since before he and Weezee parted ways, back when he'd had the PBJ sandwich. It seemed like a long time ago.

Indie reached into her small pack on the floor and pulled out a cold drink, a watermelon-peach spritzer. Bud liked this brand, though it was a bit too pricey for him, but Wilma Jean bought it occasionally.

He popped the lid—there was something printed on the underside, and he tried to read it in the dark. Indie saw what he was doing and directed the flashlight onto it.

"Better blow on outta there," it read. Bud grinned, taking a big swig.

"So, Bud, you wanna tell us why you were hiding on the floor in the Ute Tower way up on the plateau in the dark?" Junior asked.

Bud wasn't so sure he wanted Indie to know what had gone on with Annie and all, so he simply replied, "Well, I went up there so I could talk to my former deputy, Howie, since there's no cell service in the valley. He's starting a country-swing band and needed some advice. I'm his band manager. By the way, he says you're all invited to their next gig."

Junior squinted and gave Bud a sidelong look.

"When's the concert?" Indie asked innocently.

"I'm not sure," Bud replied, "but I'll keep you posted. They want to play in Paradox, if there's some place that can accommodate them."

"They could play in my back yard," she answered. "I have a big lawn, almost an acre, and a patio. It would be lovely. I could do a tofucue."

"What the hell's a tofucue?" Junior asked.

Indie gave him a dirty look, though he couldn't see her in the dark. "It's a tofu barbecue. You know, that stuff we hippie weirdos eat. That stuff that's actually good for you, good for the environment, and good for your karma, though yours is so far gone I don't think anything could rescue it at this point."

Junior grunted, and Bud tried to sidetrack the oncoming argument.

"How'd you know where I was, anyway?"

Junior replied, "Your wife called me. Why in hellsbells didn't you just call me yourself?"

"I wanted to see if the communication lines were working," Bud replied. "Plus, I didn't have time. There was someone at the door."

They drove on down the plateau in the dark, winding down a narrow dirt road that eventually dropped into the canyon and paralleled the river, then opened into the Paradox Valley.

Junior dropped Indie off at her house, then turned around and headed for the general store.

He leaned back a bit and said, "Now you can tell me the real reason you were up there, Buddy. We had a bit of a worry when the horses all came back and Weezee was there with them."

"Where is she now?" Bud asked.

"She ran into the ranch pasture with Annie's horses. Indie called me, and Joe came and picked her up. What the heck happened?"

"You been up on the plateau much, Uncle?" Bud asked in reply.

"Not much. I used to go up to Columbine Spring some for picnics when I was younger, but it's been a long time since I really spent much time up there. Why?"

"You ever seen any Ute tree burials?"

"Can't say I have."

"Well," Bud replied, "I came upon several today, and I can say it was pretty strange. Especially since the platforms were in ponderosa pines."

"What's so strange about that?"

"Ponderosas don't have much in the way of limbs. They're tall trees with short branches."

"So it would be hard to make platforms stay up there?"

"Exactly," Bud said, "unless you had a few nails to help."

With that, he pulled a nail from his shirt pocket. "These burials had a little help, like they were staged."

"Did they have bodies on them? Seems like any skeletons would be pretty much blown away or fallen by now, since the Utes haven't been practicing that custom for a long time."

"Right, at least a couple hundred years. There were skeletons, but they weren't real. They were plastic." Bud now pulled out the small yellowish-white plastic chip.

"What the heck?" Junior asked.

"I dunno, but along with everything else that happened today, this whole thing is starting to feel like a paradox."

"A paradox?" Junior asked.

"A paradox, and not the kind you find in the medical clinic or along the lakefront. The kind that says what you think is going on isn't what's really going on at all."

"Well, it would help if I had even the vaguest idea of what I thought was going on," Junior replied as they pulled up to the store and got out.

Just then, they could hear the phone inside ringing. Junior ran in and answered it as Bud waited, wanting to head for the cafe. He was starving and still thirsty. It didn't take long until Junior came back out.

"That was Indie on the phone, Buddy. She said someone left the ranch right after we did. They must've come in while we were gone. Two vehicles—an old white van and Annie's green Subaru, and she said it looked like Annie was driving."

"I'm sure they're long gone by now," Bud answered, opening the cafe door, favoring his sore left side. "I need to get some dinner. Come on in and I'll tell you about my day up on the plateau. It was kind of interesting."

With that, they went in and sat down, while LuAnn fixed them a spaghetti dinner with fresh-baked garlic bread. They then talked far into the night, long after LuAnn had locked the door and turned off the red and green flashing neon sign that read, "Paradox Cafe."

CHAPTER 17

Bud had no idea what time it was, he just knew it was early, and that woodpecker was back, hammering on the wall again.

He'd slept so soundly in Junior's bed that he didn't even recall turning over once during the night. It had a thick memory-foam mattress that must've cost a fortune, and Bud figured Junior had bought it to make up for all the nights he'd spent sleeping in boxcars when riding the rails.

Bud finally realized that what had awakened him wasn't a woodpecker, but instead was someone pounding on the store door downstairs. A voice then drifted up through the open bedroom window, "Hey Junior, come on down and open up! I ain't got all day. I need groceries!"

Bud got up and looked out the window. A rough-looking character was standing there, looking right back up at him. He was stocky with slick black hair that stood straight up, and he wore dirty tan coveralls and muddy work boots. An old beat-up blue Dodge pickup with stock racks was parked in front of the store.

"Oh, sorry, mister. Where's Junior? Say, you must be his nephew. Can you come down and open up?"

Bud wasn't sure what to say, but managed to mumble that he'd be right down, then slipped out of his Scooby Doo pajamas (a handmade gift from Wilma Jean) and into his clothes. His left side wasn't quite as sore from his fall the day before, but he still took it slow.

He went downstairs, and as he opened the door, the guy came in and introduced himself.

"I'm Boonie. Everyone calls me that cause I'm always out boondocking in the boonies. Junior knows me well. I get his wood for him every fall. Sorry to wake you up, but I'm late for getting back up on the plateau and I can't wait around. Where is Junior, anyway?"

Bud mumbled that he didn't know and for the fellow to go ahead and get his groceries and he'd check him out. Bud then went to the cooler and found a power drink and chugged it down.

He needed to wake up. He'd been dreaming he was back in Radium at Wilma Jean's old bowling alley and kept striking out. It was a very frustrating dream, because he was trying to win another belt buckle to replace the one he'd lost, and some guy there was winning them all—he had a dozen buckles, all hanging off his belt like scalps—like Ute scalps from the burial trees up on the plateau, and he looked like the picture of Mack Murphy he'd seen on the mantle.

Bud looked at the big round school clock on the store wall. It was 8:30 a.m., not really all that early after all.

He needed to make a phone call, so went behind the counter and dialed Sheriff Joe, who promptly answered. Bud asked if they'd got a coroner's report back yet, all the time watching Boonie to be sure he wasn't listening in.

Joe replied that he'd just got it the previous afternoon, and Mack had been killed by a blow to the back of his head. He then asked Bud if he was alright. He'd been worried when Weezee had come back without him.

Bud informed him that he couldn't talk right then and would call him later, but he'd seen Annie and she was alive and well.

He then dialed his home number, hoping Wilma Jean hadn't gone to the Melon Rind Cafe yet, but no one answered. He hated to call her at the cafe, as she was always busy. He'd try again later. He left a message, telling her he missed her and asking if she'd made any fresh cinnamon rolls lately.

Now Boonie was at the counter with his groceries, ready to check out. Bud had helped Wilma Jean at the cafe, so was familiar with how a cash register worked and had no trouble ringing up the groceries.

"That'll be $42.82," he informed Boonie.

"Just put it in the book," Boonie replied.

"What book?"

"It's there under the counter. Has a red cover."

Bud pulled the book out and opened it, thumbing through the pages.

Boonie said, "It's alphabetical. Look under B."

"Here it is," Bud said. "Looks like you owe a total of $178.95. I'll add this to it. Does Junior let everyone charge their groceries?"

"Far as I know," Boonie answered. "I always trade what I owe for wood, like I told you. Can't answer for what others do."

"It looks like the whole valley owes for groceries," Bud said, surprised at the extent of the book. Some people owed almost a thousand dollars! No wonder Junior wore run-down moccasins and Wranglers with frayed cuffs.

"Your uncle's a fine man," Boonie informed Bud. "I hope it runs in the family."

Bud wasn't sure if Boonie were insinuating it might not run in the family or was just talking.

Boonie continued, "I saw you riding up on the plateau yesterday, up to the burial trees. Best to stay out of others' business, is my philosophy."

"I agree," Bud answered, "in general. But what if someone's been murdered? What's your philosophy on that?"

"Murdered? Who's been murdered?"

"Mack Murphy."

Boonie seemed to soften a bit. "Old Mack was murdered? That's too bad. Man, this place can be bad sometimes. My ex-wife, Canary Kate, she told me they used to call this place hell back in the old days. The outlaws would hide out here because it was so remote, then they'd end up shooting each other, along with whoever else was in the vicinity."

"Was Mack running with the outlaws?" Bud asked.

"Those burial trees, they were part of this scheme he had."

"What scheme?"

"He was going to make this end of the plateau into an outdoor Wild West show. Take people up on horseback. He thought he'd make a fortune. I told him he was chasing a boondoggle, and the wild man would never stand for it anyway, people coming into his territory and all."

"Who exactly is the wild man?"

"He's an old prospector fellow, a big guy, stands seven-feet tall. He came up here looking for gold years ago. Everybody knows there's no gold here. He just kind of ended up going feral. Doesn't keep himself up anymore. A damn shame, watching a man turn into an animal like that."

Bud was realizing he'd discovered his own gold mine, one named Boonie. He went over to the cooler and got out an Eskimo Pie and handed it to him. "On the house," he said. "Boonie, how can a human turn into a beast?"

Boonie looked at the ice-cream bar and asked, "Mind if I trade this for a soda? Sugar gives me the jitters." He took an orange pop from the small cooler next to the counter and popped the top open, taking a swig and smacking his lips.

"A beast? I wouldn't say he's a beast. Just an unkempt old man, pretty harmless."

"But I saw a beast up there," Bud replied. "It wasn't human at all."

Boonie grinned. "Oh, you ran into the real wild man. No, he's not human. Stay away from that dude. He probably won't harm you, but he sure likes to scare people. He and I have had a couple of run ins, but he always backs off."

"What is he?"

"Hell if I know, maybe the son of Cain. That's what Canary Kate always said. She was all into reading the Bible. That's why we split up. She went to Salt Lake and joined some religious cult. Never heard from her again."

"You have any idea why someone would want to kill Mack?" Bud knew it was a long shot, but he might as well ask, since Boonie was being so talkative.

"Not me. I always liked the guy. He was pretty out of touch, but he had money, though I have no idea where he got it. He was always bringing me groceries when he came up on the plateau. I did some work for him, helped him build a few things up there for his Wild West thing, like the burial trees. At least until he reneged on the deal."

Boonie sounded angry. He dropped his empty soda can on the floor, stomped on it, smashing it flat, then handed it to Bud. "I gotta go. Five cents," he said.

"I'll take it off your bill," Bud answered.

Boonie grinned. "Come on up sometime and bring me a six-pack of that Evolution Ale that Junior keeps in the back. I'll tell you some more stories about Mack."

"I would do that," Bud answered, "if I knew where to find you."

"County Road 16, six miles off the Divide Road on the left. That's where I have my timber permit."

Just then, the phone rang. Boonie nodded goodbye to Bud, picked up his groceries, and walked out the door. Bud noticed he had a slight limp.

"Yell-ow," Bud answered.

"Buddy, you're supposed to say, 'Junior's General Store' when you answer."

It was Junior.

"I haven't had any training in this entrepreneurship thing," Bud answered. "But in spite of that, I just made you a big sale, or I should say, a big credit sale."

"Who was it?" Junior asked.

"Boonie."

"Darn. I needed to tell him to bring me some good wood this year, none of that damn aspen. It burns too fast. He still around?"

Bud looked out the window. "Nope."

"Well, OK. Buddy, I'm callin' to ask you to mind the store for me for a bit. I'm currently indisposed."

Bud wasn't sure what that meant, so said nothing.

"I'll be back in an hour or two."

CHINLE MILLER

"OK, not a problem," Bud answered. "You mind if I start charging people real money, though, so I can buy breakfast at LuAnn's?"

"She owes me a small fortune, so you get whatever you want and tell her I'll take it off her bill. But you stay there and watch the store for me. Have her run something across to you, she won't mind."

Bud badly wanted to ask his uncle where he was, but he somehow got the feeling Junior didn't want him to know.

"OK, I'm gonna order Adam and Eve on a raft. See you when you get back."

CHAPTER 18

In spite of Junior's wishes, Bud had put the "Pay at Cafe" sign up at the store and was now having breakfast across the street at the Paradox Cafe. There was no one else there except LuAnn, and she sat across from him in the booth, drinking coffee.

"Where's Junior?" she asked.

"Dunno," Bud mumbled over his eggs and toast.

"I know exactly where he is," LuAnn replied, sounding both chagrined and irritated.

Bud stopped chewing and looked at her.

"He's over at that Indie Jones's place."

"What's he doing over there?"

"Beats me," LuAnn answered. "He acts like he can't stand her in public, then goes over there all the time. I hardly see him any more. He says she's loony, but he sure seems to like hanging around her."

"He says you're loony, too."

"I know. And when he starts saying some other woman's loony, well, Bud, I just worry about that."

"Are you jealous, LuAnn?"

"Well, I never thought about it like that before, but yes, maybe you could say I am. She's too young for him, anyway."

"I bet he has some reason for being there. I don't think he's really attracted to her like that."

"How can you tell?"

"He's my uncle, I can tell."

Bud couldn't really tell anything, but he wanted to reassure LuAnn.

"I didn't realize you guys were a couple," he added, then immediately regretted saying it. LuAnn blanched.

"Well, I guess we're really not, but I sure think the world of him. I thought he did me, too."

"I know he does, LuAnn. Whatever the reason for being at Indie's, I know it has nothing to do with that."

Bud didn't know that at all, but he had trouble seeing his uncle being attracted to Indie. They were too different.

"I asked him to marry me, but he says he can't cause he might want to ride the rails again someday. Ain't that somethin'?" LuAnn looked like she was about to cry. Bud was surprised that she would share that with him.

"Maybe you should tell him you've always wanted to ride the rails yourself. I think he's just dealing with commitment-phobia. He'll never ride the rails, he's too stoved up. It's dangerous, and you have to be pretty agile to hop a freight. But I sure would welcome you to the family if you two got married. You would be really good for him."

"Well, thanks, I appreciate that, but it doesn't look very promising. And I may have to start riding the rails myself if this place doesn't pick up. Business is totally terrible. It wasn't like this before Mack started buying everyone out. Half the valley's left."

"Junior made it sound like Mack bought you out, too."

"He did, and that made Junior mad. He refused to sell the store, even though Mack made him a good offer. I could tell this place was going to hell in a hand basket, so I sold out."

"Well, then, what's the problem? Don't you have the money? Can't you just leave?"

LuAnn got up and grabbed the coffee pot, refilling their cups, then sat back down.

"No, I don't have the money yet. We had a contract, but I wanted to put it off a bit and have some time to pack up and figure out where to go. So the contract is post-dated, and I doubt if it's even binding now that Mack's dead."

Bud put some cream in his coffee and took a long sip. "Well, that makes it tough to know what to do, doesn't it? But Annie's probably going to inherit everything, wouldn't you think? Wouldn't she honor the contract?"

"Who knows? And who knows if she's even alive? And if she is, she may end up in prison for killing Mack." LuAnn looked desultory.

Bud almost told LuAnn that Annie was indeed alive, but decided to hold back. He remembered what Junior had said about the cafe being an information center, and he didn't want it to come back to haunt him. He started twirling the ends of his mustache, getting wax all over his fingers.

"Well, I know it'll all work out and be OK, LuAnn," he said. "But I guess I need to get back over to the store in case someone comes in."

"Junior's not doing so well, either," she offered.

"I wondered about that," Bud replied. "Especially after seeing that everyone charges everything."

"This whole valley's dying off. We both qualify for Social Security next year, but I don't think Junior ever paid enough into it to get anything back out."

"Yeah, one of the hazards of being a hobo."

"He and I were talking about starting a little cafe somewhere else, like maybe over in Radium, where there are more people. But if he decides to hang out with Indie, to hell with him. I sure ain't gonna sit around and wait for some guy who doesn't even appreciate my cooking."

With that, LuAnn stood and picked up Bud's empty dishes and stomped back into the kitchen. Bud stood to leave, but LuAnn came back out, carrying something.

"Here, give this to your uncle. Tell him I don't want it over here any more. He used to come over and play it every evening, but now he ain't got time for it—or me."

LuAnn handed Bud a case with the word "Noble" stamped on it in gold.

"What is it?" he asked.

"It's Junior's slide guitar." She turned and went back into the kitchen.

Bud was surprised. He had no idea his uncle played slide guitar. He slowly carried it back over the store, musing on how much he really didn't know about his uncle.

• • •

Bud had decided to clean out the ice-cream cooler and was in up to his elbows when the phone rang.

Dang, he thought, Junior gets more phone calls than he used to when he was Sheriff of Emery County.

"Yell-ow."

"Hi, Hon. Remember me?" It was Wilma Jean.

"Oh man, do I wish I was home right now."

"What's going on?"

"Oh, the same old same old, I just miss you. How're the kids?"

"Well, I told them both they were in deep trouble when you got home, assuming you decide to come back, given all the excitement over there."

"Of course I'm coming back. What happened?"

"When?"

"Whattya mean, when?"

"When are you coming back?"

"I don't know. Soon."

"Well, Hoppie and Pierre need their dad. They both managed to chew their way out the screen door yesterday. Then they went out into the yard and dug up the petunias I'd just planted."

"They're bad little doggies. No chewies for them."

"So, Hon, when are you coming home?"

"I don't know," Bud answered, exasperated. "I sure wish I'd never come over here in the first place. Well, not really, I guess, but things are just too complicated. But you'll be happy to know that the sheriff has me on as a part-time deputy, so at least I'm making some money." As he spoke, he saw Junior drive up in his old pickup.

"But Hon, I gotta go. Junior's back, and I need to talk to him. I sure miss you guys."

"Me, too, Sweetie," Wilma Jean replied as she hung up.

Just then, Junior walked in the door with a big grin on his face.

"Buddy," he said, "I think I'm gonna go be an open-air navigator again."

"What's that?" Bud asked.

"I'm gonna go ride the rails again, my boy," he answered, smiling. "With the smoke and the stars and fire at night, Up again in the morning bright, With nothing but road and sky in sight, And nothing to do but go...That's an old hobo poem. I'm leaving tomorrow and may never come back. Don't tell LuAnn, whatever you do."

CHAPTER 19

It was the next morning, and Bud was again watching Junior's store when he heard the door open. He was sitting in the easy chair by the old wood stove, fiddling with Junior's Noble slide guitar. He needed an amp to really do it right, but he could kind of hear the chords he was playing.

He was too distracted to really notice who had come in, just that is was some tall lanky guy wearing a cowboy hat.

"Howdy. Junior here?" the stranger asked.

"Nope, can't say that he is, unfortunately," Bud replied without looking up. His uncle had left that morning to go ride the rails, against Bud's better judgement.

"Mind if I get some groceries?"

"Might as well, everyone else does," Bud answered.

"You work here?"

"It's starting to look that way," Bud said.

"Well, what I mean is, can I put some groceries on my bill?"

"Sure, go ahead, everyone else does," said Bud.

Bud had played guitar a bit when he was a kid up on the Nutter Ranch with his grandpa, but he hadn't really done much with it since then. He was beginning to realize that playing a slide guitar wasn't anything like playing a regular guitar. Maybe he should get one of these to fiddle with, he thought, cause then he'd be doing something productive at the same time he was fiddling. Maybe he could even join Howie's band.

After a bit, the stranger pushed his cart up to the counter and Bud got up to go check out the groceries.

"That's $67.98," he informed the stranger.

"My name's Bodie Wilson. It should be in the book under Wilson."

Bud forgot all about the slide guitar. This must be the Bodie guy that Indie had said was Mack's hired hand. He'd been intending to go talk to him, but things kept getting in the way. He opened the book and wrote down the number, noting that Bodie now owed Junior $789.21.

"Say, I'm Bud Shumway, Junior's nephew. Nice to meet you." Bud held his hand out and shook hands with Bodie.

"Is Junior out of town or something?" Bodie asked.

"Kind of. I'm not really sure where he is at the moment."

Junior had left that morning, saying he was going to drive to Grand Junction, the nearest town with a train going through it, and hop a freight. Bud was hoping it was a flash in the pan, and he would turn around and drive back.

Bud wanted to leave, too. He'd made an agreement with Sheriff Joe that he'd stay and help solve the murder, but he really didn't see how he could solve anything while working in Junior's store.

But maybe he'd been wrong about that, he mused, if the murder suspects came to him. Everyone had to eat, so everyone would show up in the store, sooner or later.

"Say, Bodie, you ever play one of these?" Bud asked, pointing to the guitar.

"No, but Junior sure does a fine job on that one. I heard him play it once at the old grange over in Naturita. He used to have a band called the Sunshine Warblers."

"No kidding? Man, I'm finding out there's a lot I don't know about my uncle."

"He's a fine guy, and you're lucky to be related to him. I wish I had someone like him in my family."

"Where's your family?" Bud asked.

"They're all in Telluride, trying to get rich. Except my mom, and she lives over in Green River, Utah. She's the only one in the family who has any sense. She's the librarian there, not that it's much of a library, but she likes it."

"You mean Sadie Wilson's your mom? She and my wife are good friends—Wilma Jean Shumway. I live in Green River. My wife's on the library board."

"That's your wife? My mom speaks highly of her, talks about things they're doing all the time. Wow, small world."

"That's for sure. So, you work for Mack Murphy, right? Are you still taking care of things now that he's gone, or has someone else taken over?"

"I'm still taking care of everything, more than usual now, since Annie's gone. She used to at least feed the horses, but now I do all that. And I hate those damn buffalo. Murph got them to add a Western look to the place. Damn waste of money. They're mean, chased me out of the pasture the other day when I was trying to fix the hotwire."

"Indie told me Annie came back and got her car."

"She did? So that's what happened to it—I wondered. Well, I'm glad to hear she's OK. I was worried about what might have happened to her. You know, she just disappeared, along with Maggie and the horses. I'm glad the horses are back, even if it's just more work for me. Was Maggie with her? I was sure fond of that old dog. I hope she's OK."

"She had Maggie with her," Bud replied, not wanting to tell Bodie how he knew. "Say, were you around the night that Mack was killed? Did you happen to hear or see anything unusual?"

Bodie's face turned white, which was hard, given the suntan he had from being outside all the time. He sat down in another old chair and sighed.

"I'll be perfectly honest with you, Bud. Working for Mack is a full-time job, and I do mean full-time. He has a very extensive high-tech irrigation system on his fields, and if something goes wrong, I get to fix it. And I don't mean the next day, either. Everything's computerized, and when a pump goes out or something gets clogged and stops working, I'm Johnny on the spot. There are lights on the big rotary sprinklers, and I can see them from my place.

Anyway, the night Mack was killed, I'd been up late watching the Not Tonight Show and noticed one of the sprinkler lights was out. I always look over that way and check before I go to bed. I'd planted alfalfa in that particular field with a cover crop of oats, and I was babying it, keeping a close watch. It's been a dry spring and unseasonably hot.

So, I put my boots back on and tramped over there. I had just reset everything when I heard people yelling at each other. I assumed it was Annie and Murph, that's what I called Mack, and this yelling went on for awhile. I couldn't hear what was being said, but it was a man and a woman. They were inside the house, but must've had some windows open.

It finally stopped, and I went on back home, kind of upset. Annie's my friend, and she'd told me more than once she wanted to leave Paradox. She didn't like it here. She and Murph were starting to fight over it, as he didn't want her to leave. He had all these big plans for getting rich. Seems like everyone's got plans for getting rich."

"So," Bud replied, "Do you think Annie's the type to murder her own husband?"

Bodie's face got even whiter. "Good Lord, no. She's the gentlest kindest person I've ever met, other than my own mom. You may not know this, but those three horses were all rescued by her from some old rancher who wasn't feeding them. He went to jail over it. When she got them, they were just skin and bones. And Maggie came from the dog pound out in California somewhere. Annie has a good heart. Too bad she ended up with a son-of-a-gun like Murph. But at least now she'll inherit everything and be able to live where she wants. She deserves it."

Bodie stood, then added, "You know, there is one thing I forgot. That same night, I heard the weirdest sound I've ever heard. I was standing out on my porch, couldn't sleep as I was still feeling unsettled about all the yelling. This combination roar and scream came from over at Murph's place. It was so loud it made everything shake, even though it wasn't that close, like it had low frequency waves in it or something. Hard to describe, but terrifying. And it sounded like it had caused the buffalo to stampede. I went back in and locked the house up. Couldn't sleep all night, and I thought I even saw someone hiding in the bushes by my house a bit later."

"Do you think it was the wild man?" Bud asked.

"Yeah, maybe, the sound was, but the real one—not the old prospector—the real one. I heard it once a few years ago when I was up on the plateau, and I don't go up there anymore."

"I heard it up there just the other day, and I know exactly what you're talking about," Bud answered.

"Stay away from there, is my advice. I'm thinking about quitting and going somewhere else. Problem is, I don't know who to tell I'm quitting. I haven't been paid for several months, but I can't just walk off with livestock to feed and all. Thankfully your uncle lets me charge groceries or I'd have to go up on the plateau and poach deer. Anyway, gotta go. Nice talking with you, Bud."

Bodie opened the door, then turned and added, "I forgot one other thing. There's a field over there by the buffalo, and Mack told me to stay out of it. He was planting something in there he didn't want me dealing with, so I stayed away from it. From a distance it looks like maybe drugs or something. I don't know, none of my business."

He paused, then added, "And by the way, that's a nice stash you have there. Makes you look like an old-time cowpuncher. You would've fit well into Murph's plans to turn this place into the Wild West. What he didn't realize was that it once was the Wild West, the real deal, and it took a lot of good people's efforts to civilize it. Most of us prefer it civilized."

Bud watched Bodie walk out to a white Ford pickup and put his groceries in the bed. The words "Big Mack's Little Ponderosa Ranch" were painted on the side.

It was then that Bud noticed that Bodie had a slight limp.

CHAPTER 20

Bud sat back down with the steel guitar, trying to play the Red River Valley. He wasn't really paying that much attention to what he was doing, because he was really just fiddling. Something was bothering him, something he'd been puzzled about ever since he and Junior had been at Indie's house.

Indie had told them that she heard the horses thundering by in the night, but since her house was right on the fence line, there was no way the horses could have thundered by.

Either she was exaggerating, lying, or the gate was already open, which would be the only way they could thunder by, otherwise they would've had to stop while Annie or whoever was on one of them opened it.

Maybe it seemed like a minor point, but if the gate were already open, it seemed to Bud that the whole escape was preplanned. This would go with the theory that Annie had planned to kill Mack. Premeditated murder.

On the other hand, maybe the gate had been accidentally left open, but it sounded to him like the gate was always carefully closed. It was hard to tell, but Indie said the horses often got out of their pasture and it wasn't a big deal, as they couldn't get off the ranch. And even if the gate were open, Annie and the horses wouldn't know that and would've stopped anyway, thinking it was closed. Unless they'd preplanned the whole thing, that is. He figured the only reason the buffalo didn't go out it was because they didn't see it.

Bud put the guitar back into its case and went to the counter, taking out Junior's charges book. He flipped it open to the M's and looked for either Mack or Annie Murphy, but saw neither. That made sense, since they had money and wouldn't need to charge groceries.

He then flipped to the J's, where he saw Indigo Jones and the number $455.70. It looked like Indie's income wasn't doing so great, along with most of the rest of the valley, as she'd been making some major charges.

But under that number was a series of three scribbles in Junior's handwriting, each reducing the total by $60 and with a date next to it, taking the final sum owed down to $275.70. The most recent date had been yesterday, when LuAnn had said he'd been over at Indie's house.

It appeared to Bud that his uncle and Indie were doing some kind of a trade, but what could they possibly be trading? Then it occurred to Bud that maybe Junior was getting addiction counseling from her. The price seemed about right, what a therapist would charge per hour, but he couldn't picture Junior sitting there listening to anything Indie told him. Plus, his uncle would never spend that kind of money on something so intangible, and Bud had no idea what his uncle could be addicted to—he didn't smoke or drink.

Bud turned to the L's, immediately coming to LuAnn Luttrell. She owed $1,799.21.

Bud was shocked. He guessed LuAnn wasn't kidding when she said she wasn't doing so well, but surely when she bought groceries for the cafe she was able to make enough off them to repay Junior. Unless, like Junior, she too was running a charitable concern.

Bud shook his head. No wonder neither of them had any money. On the other hand, it probably didn't really matter, as it looked like the whole valley was slowly going under and there wouldn't be a store or cafe there much longer anyway. He felt a twinge of sadness. Maybe Mack's scheme would've been good for the valley in the long run.

This brought him back to his original thoughts—who would kill Mack Murphy, and why? Whoever it was, they were strong enough to kill him with some kind of a blow to the head, and that probably let Annie off the hook, as she hadn't looked overly strong to Bud. But why would she write in her little notebook that she had killed him? And why was the gate open like she'd preplanned an escape?

Bud wondered if Annie had really killed Mack. The way it was worded, maybe it wasn't a confession at all, but hypothetical. "How could I possibly kill my own husband?" But maybe she was asking herself why she did it.

It was all too confusing, and Bud went over to the cooler and got an Eskimo Pie, sitting back down in the big easy chair to eat it.

He wondered where his Uncle Junior was and if he'd made it to Grand Junction. He half expected a call later from some little railroad-town sheriff asking him to come and pick Junior up.

He had no clue what had set Junior off to want to go ride the rails again. It had been years since he'd been a hobo, and things were different now, it was a much more dangerous undertaking. And if there had ever been any glamour or adventure in it, that was probably long gone. It was a long-forgotten era—except not forgotten by Junior, that is.

Bud licked the chocolate layer off the vanilla ice cream, dropping a chunk on his tan pants. He always ate the chocolate first, then licked the ice cream into a pointy mass, chomping off the end. It was a skill he'd refined as a kid. There was a real science to eating an Eskimo Pie, he thought, or would you call it an art?

The thought that maybe his uncle had killed Mack and was running away crossed Bud's mind, but he knew it wasn't part of Junior's makeup to kill anyone, even though Junior hadn't liked Mack. He just wasn't that kind of guy. But why, out of the blue, would Junior suddenly just take off? He knew Bud wasn't really wanting to hang around Paradox and would rather be home in Green River, yet he'd abandoned him to run his store.

Bud heard the screen-door slam and looked up. It was LuAnn. It was the first time he'd seen her not wearing her waitress uniform, and she looked completely different in a light green sweater and tan slacks. Her red hair was loose across her shoulders and softened her face. Bud was surprised at how pretty she was.

"Morning, LuAnn," he said, finishing his last bite of Eskimo Pie. "You sure look nice. You going somewhere?"

"Hi Bud. Junior's not around, I take it, since his truck's gone. So much for your man's intuition that he doesn't like Indie. It looks like they ran off together."

Bud half expected her to stomp her foot, she was so angry.

"Ran off together?" Bud asked, dumbfounded.

"I saw him and Indie heading out of town early this morning."

Bud sighed. "You did? He told me he was going to go ride the rails. Why would Indie want to go ride the rails?"

"Whatever. It doesn't matter anymore. I'm outta here myself. I came to tell you goodbye."

Bud was shocked. All he could manage to say was, "Goodbye?"

"I closed the cafe and I'm leaving."

"Leaving?"

"I'm going to Telluride. My sister lives there. I'm gonna go find myself a rich man."

"LuAnn, you can't leave. I'll starve to death," Bud moaned.

"Ha," she replied. "You're standing in the middle of a grocery store. See over there? Those are eggs. And over there? Bacon. All you have to do is put them in a pan and cook them, just like I do."

"But it won't taste the same. And I could never bake an apple pie like you do, or make that gourmet spaghetti and garlic bread. You can't leave!"

"Bud, you're a lot nicer man than your uncle, that's for sure. I'll miss you."

With that, she gave him a hug, started out the door, hesitated for a moment, then turned around and took an Eskimo Pie from the cooler.

"Put it on my tab."

As LuAnn got into her car and drove off, Bud had the sinking sense that before long, the way things were going, he would be the last man in Paradox—that would be a good name for a movie, he thought.

He sat back down in the big comfy chair and began twirling the ends of his mustache, just as he saw Junior's old pickup drive up, with Indie behind the wheel and no Junior.

CHAPTER 21

"You know, Bud, my name is Indie, which is short for Indigo. I'm called that because my spiritual mentor told me I have an indigo aura. I bet you have no idea what that means, do you?"

Bud sat in the big comfy chair and nodded his head no while Indie towered above him, as much as a thin wiry woman could tower.

"An indigo aura represents a spiritual seeker, someone who's well-evolved and very patient. But I'm about to lose my patience with you. I already lost it with your uncle."

Bud got up and went and got an Eskimo Pie from the cooler, handing it to Indie. "Have a seat," he told her, pointing to the chair he'd just vacated.

Indie sat down and opened the wrapper on the ice cream. "I haven't had one of these for years," she said. "I usually don't eat junk food."

"One every few years or so won't hurt you," Bud replied. "But Indie, I can't believe you would aid and abet my uncle in being irresponsible."

"If I hadn't given him a ride, his old truck would be sitting there at the railroad yard and eventually be towed. Besides, I'm encouraging him to mature and grow by reliving his past and resolving old issues. Maybe you'd like to start getting therapy, too?" She raised her eyebrows.

"I thought maybe you were counseling him," Bud replied, "But for some reason, I can't picture it, my uncle going to a therapist, and not just any therapist, but you."

Indie's eyes flashed. "What do you mean by that?"

"I mean, you and my uncle are about as different as can be in world views. You know that."

"The mark of a mature evolved human being is the ability to consider different viewpoints. Junior's making some progress, though he has a long ways to go, I admit." Indie began licking the chocolate layer off the Eskimo Pie.

Bud continued, "Are you making any progress?"

"With Junior?"

"No, with seeing different viewpoints."

Indie shot him a look. "That's my area of expertise," she replied. "That's what therapists do."

"Really? Then why are you trying to change my uncle? I happen to like him as he is. You've somehow convinced him he needs help."

"Look, Bud, you really are trying my patience," Indie answered. "I'm an addiction counselor. Your uncle came to me. He has an addiction he wants me to help him with."

"What in the world could he be addicted to? Tea? Oneryness?"

"I'm not at liberty to discuss my clients' personal matters," she answered. "But I will say that it's made his life very difficult, and he wants to change it. It has to do with LuAnn, and I can't say any more about it."

"LuAnn? She just left."

"What? She left?" Indie stood, visibly upset. "That's not part of the plan. She can't leave! Where did she go?"

"Telluride. It's OK, Indie, there's lots of groceries here in the store. You won't starve."

"Listen, Buster, this isn't about me. LuAnn's part of the plan. If she leaves, Junior will just regress backwards. I'm beginning to see some progress and that will just end it."

Bud could now see someone driving up. He knew he was running out of time and quickly asked, "Indie, speaking of leaving, I know you helped Annie with her little plot. And I know you know where she is. I really need to talk to her—it's in her own best interest."

"What? Helped Annie with her plot? What plot?" Indie was now furious. "Are you accusing me of helping murder Mack?"

"Was that Annie's plot?" Bud asked quietly.

The vehicle doors slammed, and Bud knew the conversation was about to end.

"I can't believe you would think that about Annie," Indie said, "or about me."

"You lied on her behalf, didn't you, Indie?"

"Lied about what?"

Just then, Carl and Jimmy entered the store, the screen door slamming behind them.

Bud finished. "Just get me in touch with Annie, that's all I ask. If she's innocent, there's no need to hide."

With that, Indie walked out, looking pale, the screen door slamming behind her.

● ● ●

"You need to talk to Annie?" Jimmy asked. "We can get you in touch with her. She's down at the old hot springs."

Carl gave him a dirty look. "We weren't supposed to tell anyone, remember?"

"Bud's not just anyone, he's a P.I. We're on his side, remember?"

Bud opened the cooler and handed them each an Eskimo Pie. It was about time to order more, he thought, though he had no idea where to get them.

"Why's she hiding out?" Bud asked. "Why not just go home?"

Carl answered, "Dunno, none of our business."

"She has Maggie with her, right?"

"Yeah," Jimmy answered. "She's one cool old dog—Maggie, not Annie." He was now licking the chocolate off the ice cream bar, turning it round and round.

"Did Annie come to you guys for a ride up to the Ute Tower?" Bud asked.

"No, we saw her walking down the road by the ranch and gave her a ride, then we took her home where she got her car," Jimmy replied.

"How'd you know we gave her a ride?" Carl asked suspiciously.

"Give it up, Carl, he's a P.I.," Jimmy answered, whacking Carl on the shoulder. "But we need to get some supplies, Mr. Shumway. We're going back up to look for gold. That's a secret, though you probably already figured it out."

Carl gave Jimmy another dirty look, to which Jimmy said, "What? What? He's not gonna tell anyone. He's a P.I."

The phone was ringing, so Bud said, "You guys go ahead, and I'll check you out when you're ready." He then picked up the receiver.

"Yell-ow."

It was Howie. "Hey Sheriff, that you?"

"Last I noticed," Bud said.

"Well, I need your advice. I'm sorry the only time I ever call is when I need your help. One of these days I'm gonna call and just talk, that would be a surprise, eh?"

Bud acknowledged to himself that it would indeed be a surprise for Howie to call and just talk. He waited, knowing it did no good to ask Howie why he was calling.

"You still there?" Howie asked.

"Still here, Howie. Good to hear from you."

"Thanks and likewise, but I need your advice."

"Go ahead, Howie."

"Say, Sheriff, you seem kind of put off. I'm not interrupting anything, am I?"

"No, no, Howie, you're fine."

"OK, good. Anyway, we found ourselves a bass player—that guy you recommended. He's pretty good, can play country just fine, but he's wanting to play a song that I think might be a bit offensive, and I'm not sure what to do. He's from Chicago, you know. I don't want to offend him by worrying about being offensive, if you know what I mean."

"Well, no, you sure don't want to offend anyone. What's it called?"

"He wrote it—I'm not sure what he calls it. It's got a great tune, but the lyrics are about a hobo guy riding in a reefer, and I sure don't want anyone to think we condone drugs, Bud."

"A reefer? Are you thinking that's marijuana, Howie?"

"Well, isn't it?"

"How could you ride in marijuana?" Bud asked.

"I dunno, I thought maybe it was symbolic or something."

Bud grinned. "Howie, a reefer is a refrigerated truck. But if you think that might be misinterpreted, just change it to something like riding in a boxcar or an 18-wheeler or something else. Might be a bit warmer for the poor hobo, too."

Howie sounded relieved. "Oh man, Sheriff, I sure feel dumb. But I knew you could straighten things out. Thanks a million."

"No problem, Howie. Say, I think I found a venue for you guys to play over here in Paradox."

"A what?"

"A venue, you know, a place for a concert."

Now Howie sounded excited. "No kidding?"

"Yeah, let me know when you plan on coming over, and we can get things rolling."

"Oh, man, Sheriff, I dunno, it seems pretty soon. I mean, we just kinda got going." Howie sounded nervous.

"There's no hurry, just when you're good and ready."

"Well, thanks. I'll tell Maureen and Barry, he's our new bass player. When you coming back?"

"I dunno. Soon, I hope."

"Well, OK, gotta run. Thanks again. 10-4, over and out."

Bud hung up the phone just as Carl and Jimmy walked up with a cart of groceries.

"What name do you want this under?" Bud asked.

"Name? No name, we always pay cash," Carl answered, handing his Eskimo Pie stick to Jimmy and pulling out his wallet.

"OK, but I hope I can make change," Bud replied.

CHAPTER 22

"Can I help you? Maggie acts like she knows you," Annie asked.

The old dog stood at Bud's side, licking his hand and wagging her tail. He was at the old Fountain of Youth Hot Springs, which had several run-down seedy looking rooms attached to the main building, which was closed. It sat on the very edge of the valley, near an old closed uranium mine, and looked deserted and about to fall down. And, as if to add their special touch to the scene, Bud noted a flock of buzzards circling overhead.

Annie was very pretty, Bud noted, tall and thin with her blonde hair pulled back into a ponytail, but not wiry like Indie. She had that look about her that the well-heeled have, even though she was a bit unkempt and her clothes wrinkled. Maybe it was the expensive sunglasses and the sparkling white teeth—so white they looked kind of un-natural.

"I've come to get something that belongs to me. I'm Bud Shumway, Junior's nephew." Bud held out his hand.

Annie shook hands with him, and Bud noted she had a pretty good grip, like someone used to doing outdoor work. He knew she was a horsewoman and spent a lot of time outside. Or had, anyway.

"I can't imagine what I would have that would belong to you," Annie replied, looking puzzled. "And how did you know where to find me?" Her eyes then narrowed. "You're that private investigator guy, aren't you?"

"I'm working on a murder case, yes, although I'm more of a melon farmer by nature. But you have a belt that belongs to me. It was tied around Maggie's collar."

"Oh, that's yours?" Annie said. "Hang on a minute." She went into the room, then came back with the belt.

"How in the world did it get tied to Maggie's collar?" she asked.

"I was up on the plateau and found Maggie and didn't want to lose her. She led me to the tower."

"So, you're the one who broke the door down?"

"No, it was someone much larger than me," Bud replied.

"Oh my God," Annie gasped. "I was afraid of that. I knew I had to get out of there."

"Good move," Bud said. "But why don't you just go home? Much nicer than here, and Bodie needs a paycheck."

"I can't," Annie replied.

"The sheriff knows you're here, if that's what you're worried about. Or will know, if he happens to ask me."

"No, it's not that...and no, I didn't kill Mack."

"Then why did you write what you did in your little notebook?"

Annie looked irritated. "Look, I don't have to talk to you. You have no right to go snooping around in my stuff. Let's just call it a day. Goodbye." She turned to go back into the little motel room.

"Annie, you can talk to me, or you can talk to the sheriff. It's up to you."

"Why should I talk to you?"

"Because I'm a commissioned deputy. And you know you have the right to call your attorney and all that. But if you didn't kill Mack and you feel like you're in danger, maybe I can help you. If you did kill your husband, cooperating now will save you a lot of grief later and make you look a lot better when the sentencing comes. It's your call."

"Are you really a lawman?" she asked.

"Yup. Sheriff Joe Masters hired me to work on this case. I used to be a sheriff over in Utah."

"The guys said you were a P.I."

"I was when I talked to them. That was before I was deputized."

"Who were you working for as a P.I.?" Annie asked.

"Nobody. My Uncle Junior asked me to come over and see if I could figure things out, that's all. That was before Mack was killed. I sometimes dabble a bit in detective work when the melon farming is slow."

"Junior's really your uncle? You're really a melon farmer?"

"Yes, but look, I'm the one supposed to be asking all the questions. Maybe Joe should deputize you, as you seem to be better at it than I am."

Annie turned to go back in. "I have to go. I don't want to be seen."

"Who are you hiding from, Annie?" Bud asked gently. "Is whoever killed Mack after you, too?"

"I thought you said I killed him."

"I don't think you have it in you—mentally or physically."

"How did Mack die?" Annie looked like she was about to cry.

"Annie, I can't share that with you because it's an ongoing investigation. But just let me say that he never saw it coming."

Now Annie was crying. "He wasn't a bad person. He was just all caught up in this crazy scheme he had. And now he's gone."

"Were you and him having a big fight?"

Annie closed her eyes. "No."

"Then why all the shouting that night?"

She opened her eyes in surprise. "Who told you about that?"

"Someone who heard it. It seems Mack was having an argument with you right before he was killed. Were you arguing about leaving?"

"No, it wasn't me. I wasn't even there." Annie looked Bud right in the eyes. "Who told you that, Bodie?"

Bud ignored her question. "Where were you?"

"I was over at Indie's."

"So, you have an alibi then?" Bud asked.

"No. Indie wasn't home."

Bud was beginning to feel like a kid on a merry-go-round.

"Where was she?" he asked.

"She was over at my house, arguing with Mack."

"Why was she arguing with Mack?"

"She didn't like the way he was treating me. He didn't listen to anyone but her, and usually not even her, but she hoped he'd listen for once. But she would never kill Mack."

"Did you get Bodie to kill Mack, Annie?"

Bud figured she wouldn't admit it if she had, but he wanted to see her reaction. It was indeed possible Bodie had killed Mack, as he was certainly strong enough to hit him a stiff blow to the head. On top of that, the facts fit—he could drive a backhoe, he had a limp, and he was in the general area at the time. How far Bodie would go with helping Annie was anyone's guess.

Annie turned her back to Bud. "That's it. Go away."

She started back into the motel when Bud said, "It's not personal, Annie. It's my job—I have to ask. And are you wanting to have a funeral? Time's running out."

"No, nobody would come, anyway. I want him cremated."

"I'll have to get the papers and have you sign them. You gonna be here for awhile?"

"I don't know. I can't let anyone know where I am. You can't tell anyone."

"I won't, but I can't answer for Carl and Jimmy. Is there anything you want from your house? Where's your car, by the way?"

"It's hidden in the old garage here. Mack owns this place now, and I just happened to know where he kept the keys."

"Annie, I think you own this place now. What about groceries?"

Annie looked surprised, then said, "Carl and Jimmy brought me some. I own it? It's not even a real hot springs, just a big old swimming pool they heated up. It's all cracked now."

"Aren't you Mack's heir? You were his next of kin, his wife."

"I guess. I suppose so. You mean, I own the ranch now and everything?"

"I would think so, unless he left it to someone else. Any kids?"

"No, just me. I guess I just never thought about it. I've been too busy trying to process everything that's happened."

"Well, I would say you're one wealthy gal about now. I'll be back when I get the papers."

Bud took his little notebook from his jacket pocket and wrote down Junior's number, handing it to her.

"Here, you can reach me at Junior's store. And how about finding some means of paying Bodie before he abandons everything? A man's gotta eat. So do your horses and all those buffalo, and I sure don't want to have to start feeding them, like my uncle's doing with the rest of the valley."

"There's a checkbook in the big rolltop desk in Mack's office. Bring it and I'll write him a check."

"OK. I'd bring you an Eskimo Pie, too, but they're all gone," Bud said.

Annie looked perplexed. "What?"

"Never mind. I'll be back."

Annie and Maggie retreated back into the motel room as Bud got into his FJ. He drove back to the store, mystified at the whole chain of events.

He had no clue what was going on, and all he really wanted about now was a nice big hamburger with curly fries, as he hadn't had much for breakfast. Junior had some of those little strawberry toaster thingies that he'd seen advertised on Scooby Doo, but they were pretty unfulfilling.

He started for the Paradox Cafe, then remembered that LuAnn was gone. He guessed he'd either have to do without or make his own meal. He couldn't help but feel a bit miffed at his uncle for leaving, and he also felt that Junior was somehow responsible for LuAnn leaving.

He wondered if his uncle were riding in some empty boxcar about now. If so, Bud half-hoped Junior was hankering for a nice big hamburger with curly fries, as it would serve him right.

As he drove up to the store, he took the "Pay at Cafe" sign from the window, hoping no one had come by and wanted groceries while he was gone.

Sure enough, there on the counter was a note that read, "Bought $87.99 in groceries plus whatever the tax is. Cafe closed. Please charge. Thx. Susie Turner."

Bud groaned. This was Susie, the wife of Mack's wealthy neighbor, Tom Turner, the one he'd overheard talking on the phone to Junior, the one Junior had said knew something more than he was letting on.

Were they broke, too? If so, things were getting desperate.

He put the sign back up and got back into his FJ. It was time to pay the Turners a visit.

CHAPTER 23

Bud pulled out from in front of the general store and started down the road towards the Turner ranch. Then suddenly, on a whim, he turned towards the river instead. He was curious to know if the backhoe was still in the river.

Sheriff Joe had asked that nothing be touched until the CBI could examine everything, and that included the backhoe, but Bud knew how expensive a machine it was, and he hated seeing it sitting there in the water.

As he pulled up to the rafting takeout, he saw something that made him cringe—the backhoe was not only still in the river, but it was now on its side. He got out of the FJ and stood on the river bank.

Had the river risen during the night and moved the backhoe? He looked at the sand along the banks—no, it wasn't wet like it would be if the water had come up. Besides, it would take a flash flood to turn the machine over like that.

He now walked up and down the bank, looking for tracks, but found only what looked like geese or maybe heron tracks. Whoever had tipped the hoe over, they had to have come from the other side. But it would take another backhoe or big machine to turn it on its side like that, and there was no road over there, just thick willows. And why would anyone bother to drive into the river and tip it over, risking their own machine? Bud knew that the CBI had already examined it for fingerprints, so it would be too late to try to hide any evidence.

Bud was perplexed. He got back into the FJ and drove back over to the general store, wishing the valley had cell service, as he needed to make a phone call. He got out, went into the store, and dialed Sheriff Joe over in Telluride.

The dispatcher answered and patched Bud over to Joe's office. Bud wondered what it would be like to work for a county that had an actual dispatcher. He'd had to answer his own phone when he was sheriff over in Green River, unless Howie was around, and even sometimes when Howie was around and buried in some detective magazine.

"Sheriff Joe Masters speaking."

"Howdy, Sheriff. Bud here. Say, you know why the back-hoe in the river over here would now be tipped over?"

"Tipped over? What in the world?"

"No tracks or anything, just tipped over. Any idea yet what the CBI found?"

"Not much of anything. No fingerprints. Nothing on the hoe. One small spot of blood on the ranch where Mack was when he was killed," Joe replied.

"Is it OK now to get that thing out of the river? It's an expensive piece of machinery—or was."

"Yeah, I was going to call you later. Go ahead and get it out. You'll have to get Sammy's Towing up in Naturita. Making any progress on anything over there?"

"There's been some motion, but it's not forward. LuAnn closed down the cafe and left."

"No kidding? Where'd she go?"

"Over your way. If you see her, send her home. I'm losing weight fast."

"Well, no offense, but I think you'll survive awhile. But say, I forgot to tell you something. I got another call from the coroner over in Montrose yesterday afternoon, and he found something of interest. He said he missed it the first time around, but decided to take another look, as he didn't think the blow was hard enough to kill Mack, and he was right. What really killed him was an incision at the base of his neck, up under his hairline."

"An incision? What would make that?" Bud asked.

"He wasn't sure, but said it looked like he'd been stabbed with something—but not a knife—something with a sharp point that didn't flare like a knife."

"I'll be darned," Bud replied. "Could a spear do that?"

"Maybe," Joe answered.

"Did he find any metal or wood shards?"

"Nothing. It was as clean as could be."

"Well," Bud said, "There's a mystery for you."

"One I'm hoping you can solve, Bud. Keep me posted if anything turns up."

"That's a big can do," Bud replied, hanging up the phone.

He sure could use an Eskimo Pie about now, he thought, heading back out the door, wondering where he could order more.

It didn't take long to get to the Turner's ranch, as it sat across the road from Mack's place. As he drove by, Bud noted Indie's Honda was in front of her house, but he didn't see any signs of activity anywhere.

As Bud came to the Turner's place, he noted they had a pole gate even bigger than Mack's, with even fancier metal lettering surrounded by a big herd of metal horses that read "Turner's El Rancho Not So Grande." If this was their rancho not so grande, he wondered what their rancho grande looked like.

He drove up a long straight drive that ended in front of a huge two-story log house that looked like it had been transplanted from a national park somewhere, one of the big old lodges like he'd seen in Yellowstone and Glacier when he and Wilma Jean had gone there on their honeymoon. The only problem was, the Turner's place just rose up out of nowhere. It lacked a sense of proportion and struck one as having been built by someone who had more money than taste.

Bud got out, wondering what it would be like to have the money to build that kind of place. A big perfectly manicured green lawn surrounded the house, and pine trees had been planted in orderly rows around it, rows that looked unnatural, kind of like Annie's white teeth.

A flock of band-tailed pigeons sat in the trees, cooing, and around the property's perimeter he noticed what looked like a small railroad track.

Bud walked up the wide stairs onto the landing, which was accented by logs that had been carved into squirrels and raccoons. He stood there for a moment, twirling his mustache and kind of feeling like he was about to enter a cathedral, then rang the front doorbell.

It sounded like a cow mooing, which caught him by surprise, and he couldn't help but smile, a smile that was reflected by the face of the woman who opened the door, almost as if she'd been standing right there, waiting.

Bud said, "Afternoon, I'm Bud Shumway, Junior's nephew. Are you Mrs. Turner?"

"Oh honey, you're Junior's nephew? Well, come on in!" The petite woman had a southern accent and wore a purple knit pantsuit, something Bud hadn't seen since he was a kid and his Aunt Mattie came to visit from Salt Lake City. Over the pantsuit was a long apron that had a smiling cow on the front and the words, "Steer your way to Turner's Beef Barbecue."

"Come on back into the kitchen, Bud, I'm making a big pan of lasagna for dinner, and it's almost done. Why don't you join us?"

Bud immediately felt comfortable. He followed the woman, who he guessed must be Susie, through a huge two-story living room with a full-height stone fireplace surrounded by the mounted heads of cattle—not deer or elk or antelope, as some would have—but various shades of red and brown and white and black cattle, some with spots.

Susie noticed his interest and said, "They're not real, but paper mache. Tommy has a warped sense of humor, as your uncle's probably already told you. He had some artist in Baton Rouge make them, that's why they have such weird eyes, she apparently had never seen a cow. I don't care for them, myself."

Bud grinned. The cows did look a little cock-eyed, and one had a strong resemblance to his Uncle Junior.

"That one was modeled after your uncle," Susie said, nodding. "He and my husband Tommy are good friends. In fact, Tommy's the one who encouraged Junior to go into politics and funded his campaign chest."

"He did?" Bud asked, surprised. Junior hadn't seemed very enthralled with Tom Turner when he'd called on the phone the other night.

"Junior was over here one night having dinner and he and Tommy got into a big argument over the role of government. They argue all the time. Of course, Tommy's just as bad as Junior about the whole thing, hates the government, but they were arguing about something or other, and Tommy challenged Junior to run for mayor. He donated $200 for advertising."

"Where would you advertise around here?" Bud asked.

"That's a good point," Susie replied.

They were now in a huge kitchen that appeared to have every gadget known to humankind, including a big Viking stove and a huge Sub Zero refrigerator that Bud figured must weigh half a ton. He had always wondered why anyone would want to freeze anything that cold—it seemed to him that anything below 32 degrees would work fine.

Susie pulled a big pan of tasty-smelling lasagna from the oven, then began making a salad while talking.

"Junior bought a big chest of ice cream sticks and gave them out to everyone who came into the store, telling them to vote for him. It must've worked."

"That's pure bribery," Bud grinned. "But it sounds like my uncle. At least he was open about it."

Susie had finished tossing the salad and asked, "What kind of wine do you like with lasagna?"

She opened an under-the-counter Sub Zero wine cooler, displaying more wine bottles than Bud had ever seen—more than in the State Liquor Store in Green River, which consisted of a locked display case in the East Winds Truck

Stop that held a couple of bottles of Boones Farm wine, one of whiskey, a bottle of Bailey's Irish Creme, and some 3.2-percent beer.

"What do you recommend?" he asked, wondering how he was going to drink frozen wine.

"How about this nice 1978 bottle of Australian Shiraz?" she asked. "With Shiraz, you want to drink only the aged stuff because of the heavy tannins."

Bud nodded his head in agreement, even though he'd never even heard of Shiraz, yet alone tried it. "Sounds lovely," he said.

"Not the same as Petite Sirah. Tommy always swears it is, but it's not," she added. "Petite Sirah's a different grape, more purple and rounder in the mouth."

"Anyone with any sense knows the difference," Bud concurred.

"Well, nobody ever said my husband has any sense, and speak of the devil," she said as Tom entered the room.

Tom was tall and wore what someone from Arkansas might construe as cowboy clothing—starched-looking Levis, a red plaid shirt with mother-of-pearl buttons, red inlaid cowboy boots with extra-pointy toes, and a red handkerchief tied around his neck. Bud noticed he had a slight limp.

Tom held out his hand. "Howdy. I'm Tom Turner. You must be Junior's nephew, Buddy. How's Junior?"

Bud shook hands with him, not sure how Tom knew who he was, then figured the odds of guessing would be pretty good, as there was no one else visiting the valley that he knew of.

"To be honest, I don't know," he replied. "Last I heard, he was riding the rails."

"That rascal!" Tom said. "I bet that's who tried to call me collect from some jail early this morning. Had no idea who it was, so I refused the call. Hope he's not in trouble somewhere."

"Me, too," Bud groaned, as they all sat down to dinner. "Though it sounds like he is."

"And I bet you're here to ask if I murdered Mack Murphy," Tom said congenially as he passed Bud the lasagna.

CHAPTER 24

Bud ducked his head and grabbed onto his cowboy hat just as he and Tom entered the tunnel. Tom laughed, yelling, "I forgot to tell you to watch your head, but it's not as low as it looks."

Tom was obviously enjoying being the engineer of the small railroad, a replica of an old-time steam train, complete with an engine and caboose, with several cars in between, all painted bright red. As they exited the short tunnel, he pulled a lever that sounded the engine's whistle and a pair of grouse took to the air.

They rounded a curve that led away from the big grassy yard and over by the buffalo pasture on Mack's place. The herd of buffalo raised their heads when they saw the train coming, then bolted to the far fence.

"Those dumb buffalo run every time this train comes by. You'd think they'd get used to it," Tom yelled over the engine noise, blowing the whistle again. "Mack used to get mad at me for stampeding them, but for Pete's sake, I'm on my own land."

He pointed to a line of posts with yellow tape that bordered his side of the pasture. "They broke through several times and messed up my lawn, plus they're scary animals, so I had to put up a big hotwire. I told Mack if they came over here again I was going to put buffalo burgers on my restaurant menu."

Now Tom gunned it, and the railroad zipped along a straight stretch. He slowed down and came back to the small building that housed the train, where he stopped and cut the engine.

He just sat there, a big smile on his face. Bud thought he looked like a big overgrown kid, and wondered if he himself looked that way.

"You look like a big overgrown kid," Tom said, "with that silly grin on your face."

"That was fun," Bud answered. "Too bad Junior didn't just come up here when he got wanderlust and ride around for a bit until it went away."

"Well, he and I have spent many hours riding this silly thing around in a big circle, but I don't think his wanderlust will ever go away. That's the main thing he and I have in common, we love trains. We're both stuck with it."

"And he may very well be stuck in jail as we speak," Bud replied. "Which is a little harder to wander away from."

Tom replied, "Say, before I forget, Susie got some groceries today and there was nobody there, so she charged them. Could you put this in the till?" He handed Bud some money.

They both sat on the engine for a bit, watching the sunset, until Bud asked, "Would you mind telling me if you heard anything the night Mack died?"

Tom didn't hesitate. "Sure. I was sitting out on the front porch, watching the stars and thinking about things, something I do a lot lately, since we're leaving soon. Won't have a view like this of the night sky much longer."

Bud was surprised. "Leaving soon?"

"Like about everyone else in the valley, we sold out to Mack. He made us an offer we couldn't refuse. He really wanted this place, partly because it borders his, but also because he wanted the big house for his new headquarters."

"Headquarters?"

"Yeah, for his big development. He was going to have a Wild West thing here in Paradox, get lots of tourists and fix the economy. Problem is, it wouldn't fix the economy for anyone but Mack Murphy, cause everyone else was going to have to leave."

"Who would he hire to work on it, if everyone's gone?"

"I asked him and he just said it wouldn't be a problem."

"Did you or anyone else ever see his master plan? Or did he have one?"

"Never saw it. Not something he was going to share, I don't think, except maybe with his neighbor there, Indie Jones. She was pretty tight with him."

"How so?" Bud asked.

"Oh, they were like peas in a pod. She somehow got herself into the position of being his advisor. He couldn't do anything by himself, always had to ask Indie."

"Did his wife object to that?"

"Annie? I don't know, but she and Indie were good friends, so I doubt it. Where is she, anyway?"

"She says she's not coming back to the ranch in the near future. Would you have any idea why?"

Tom gave Bud a look. "Me? How would I know something like that? I barely know her. Maybe she's worried she'll be the next one to go."

"It kind of sounds like you and Mack weren't on the best of terms."

"Mack resented me coming in here and building all this. I managed to buy the land before he came in, or he would've been able to buy it. He said I was a poser. He thought my cowboy clothes were silly, and so what if they are? He wore a big ten-gallon hat that made him look ridiculous.

It was ironic, because he was from eastern Canada himself. He sure as hell wasn't any more of a Westerner than I was. Neither of us fit in here, it's a cultural thing. Me, I just run with it and have fun, but Mack really wanted to be accepted by the locals, which he never was. Even if you lived here 30 years they wouldn't accept you—you have to be born here—except Junior, and they like him."

"So, what happened when you were out on the porch that night?"

"I was sitting there and it was real quiet. I could see down to their ranch house, and everything seemed normal, though it kind of sounded like somebody was yelling, but I couldn't tell for sure. But all of a sudden, those damn buffalo were running around like crazy. Something had stampeded them. They're pretty flighty, but not usually like that at night when they bed down. The next morning I noticed they'd broke down the fence yet again and some were over here, so I had to round them up."

"How did you do that?"

"Oh, it's easy. I just get in the train and blow the whistle and they run back home. But I had to fix up the fence again. And this time, I fixed up Mack's fence, cause they broke that down, too, and were running all over his ranch before they came over here.

I couldn't get ahold of anybody over there, so I fixed it all up. I'm a good neighbor, though Mack never appreciated me much. Not many people would risk their lives rounding up buffalo for someone who doesn't even like them."

"Did you see any cars coming or going or anything unusual?"

"No, not a thing, except later that night I heard someone fire up the backhoe, which I thought was strange. It was sometime in the middle of the night. We sleep with the windows open and I could hear it pretty clearly."

"Did you hear a weird howling?"

"Actually, now that you mention it, I did. I kind of forgot about that. It was over in that direction, and it made my hair stand on end. I went back inside and shut the windows. But that was long before I heard the backhoe, about the same time I heard the buffalo."

Bud sat there awhile. Finally, he asked, "You could hear the backhoe with the windows closed?"

Tom laughed. "You don't miss a thing, do you? No, I doubt if I could've heard it, but it was stuffy, and Susie got up later and opened the windows again. She hadn't heard the weird howling."

A meadowlark whistled from a small nearby bush. Bud had always liked meadowlarks, and he could imitate their whistle, so he whistled back. The bird replied.

Finally, Bud asked, "Do you know any reason someone would want to kill Mack?"

Tom replied, "Sure, lots of people would. He was buying up the valley and changing everything. People didn't have the money to refuse him, as the economy's so bad here, yet they resented him changing things. He was paying good money for everything and driving up the taxes, and the assessor knew values were going up. Plus Mack was loaded, and that made people even more resentful."

"Where'd he get his money?"

"I made mine in the restaurant business, but Mack made his as a developer. He built big resorts all over the place, many which I'm sure you've heard of—ski areas, golf courses, you name it.

So then he goes and marries Annie, who I've heard is one of the greenest people on the planet, and he starts acting like he's ashamed of what he did. I'm not one to pass judgement, but then he turns around and decides to develop the valley. It's no wonder she wanted to leave him. Maybe it was like living with a recovering alcoholic who falls back off the wagon again."

"You know anything about that?" Bud asked.

"I do. I was once one myself."

Bud apologized, "I'm sorry. I wasn't asking about your personal life, I was asking if you knew anything about Annie wanting to leave Mack. I did wonder why you didn't have any wine with dinner, though."

Tom replied, "It's OK. I don't have any secrets. Sometimes telling people I was once an alcoholic helps them. And I noticed you never drank yours. I take it you're not a wine connoisseur?"

Bud laughed. "I think it's an acquired taste—one I have yet to acquire. I didn't want to offend Susie, but I just couldn't drink it."

"Well, I can tell you one thing, she's going to be offended if we don't get back in there and have some of her apple cobbler with ice cream for dessert."

Bud was the first one off the engine, but stopped cold in his tracks when Tom added, "And I forgot to mention that I saw Indie, she was the one who started up that backhoe and drove it off."

"How do you know it was her?" Bud asked.

"It was a moonlit night, and I saw her come out from the house. There's no mistaking that frizzy blonde hair."

Bud paused, then asked, "How could you see her when you were in bed?"

Tom's face turned red. "I had to get up to take a pee, something that happens all too often when you get to be my age. I'm in the habit of looking out the bedroom window when I get up, sort of a visual check of everything.

I saw Indie come out of Mack's house, and I watched for awhile, but she disappeared, so I went back to bed. It wasn't long after that I heard the backhoe start up. I got up and looked again, but it was gone. It had to be Indie."

"But you didn't actually see her get onto it?"

"Well, no, not actually."

Bud shrugged, then followed Tom back into the house.

CHAPTER 25

Bud opened the door to his FJ and crawled in, so stuffed he wasn't sure he would still fit. He had really enjoyed the evening at the Turner's, especially the dinner part, even though he'd had to suffer a bit when Tom decided to get out his slideshow of old train engines.

But Susie had finally noticed the glazed look in Bud's eyes and said enough was enough and shut it down. Bud now knew who wore the pants in the family—or the pant-suit.

Even though it was now late, he wanted to get Annie's checkbook and save himself another trip in the morning, so he turned under the Big Mack's Little Ponderosa Ranch sign, noting the lights at Indie's house were out. He pulled up in front of Mack and Annie's house and got out.

Bud couldn't see a thing, so he pulled his little flash-light from his pocket and searched for the house key under the front mat, the least likely place a burglar would look, since nobody's dumb enough to put a key there. Or at least, that's what Joe had told him when they were investigating the murder and had found the key there.

Bud carefully unlocked the big wooden front door, and just like in the horror movies, it creaked as it slowly swung open, accentuating the loneliness of the house. He fumbled a bit for a light switch and soon the living room was lit up by a huge antler chandelier.

Bud looked around, and everything looked just like it had last time he'd been there. It was a beautiful house, kind of a country style with light oak floors and sparse furnishings and a big veranda out on the back that looked out over the alfalfa fields.

A number of beautiful paintings of various types of birds hung on the wall, each bearing Annie's signature. Unlike the Turner's mansion, this place seemed more suited to the valley and was very tastefully done. He sensed Annie's hand here, the hand of someone with an artistic eye.

Bud headed to the back bedroom that served as Mack's office and searched though a stack of papers on the big rolltop desk, looking for the checkbook Annie needed. He paused when he came to a receipt. It was from the Utah State Prison in Draper, some $2350 dollars for an unspecified item.

Bud paused, wondering what in the heck one bought from a state prison. It looked like an official receipt, not like something an inmate would conjure up for something illegal, but you never know, he thought. He put it in his pocket.

Bud quickly found the checkbook, then was back out the door and in the FJ, key replaced and lights out. He was uncomfortable being in the house and didn't dally.

As he drove by Indie's house, he noticed a light was now on. Someone stood in the open door, watching as he drove up the lane.

He was going to stop, but he didn't want to tell Indie he was on an errand for Annie, as he had promised Annie not to reveal anything about her, so he kept driving.

Sure enough, it was Indie. She yelled when she saw it was Bud, but he just tapped his horn and kept going. He knew she would be irritated, especially since he himself had told her to keep an eye on the place, but he wasn't in the mood to talk to her, nor to have to make up some story as to why he was there.

He was soon back to the dark unlocked store, where, just as he flipped on the lights, the phone began ringing. Bud was pretty sure he knew who it was, and sure enough, he did.

"Bud, what were you doing over at Annie's house? I'm supposed to be watching out for everything, yet you just blaze on by here with no explanation for anything, honking at me like I'm one of your buddies on the street." Indie sounded furious.

"You mean you're not my buddy?" Bud asked.

"Look, you're trying to divert me. I want to know what you were doing over there."

"Indie, I'm a crime investigator, that's what I was doing over there."

"No, that's the job of the sheriff. You're not gonna get me that easily," she replied, still angry.

"Well. I work for the sheriff, so I do what he says," Bud answered.

This caught Indie by surprise. "You work for the sheriff? Since when?"

"Since he hired me, Indie. And I'm glad you're doing such an exemplary job of keeping an eye on everything. I'll be sure to let Sheriff Masters know. Have you seen anything unusual?"

"Just you. What were you looking for over there?"

"Nothing. I needed a drink of water and was nearby."

"At this time of night? You really scared me when I saw your lights."

"I'm really sorry, Indie, but a man never knows when he might get thirsty. I would've stopped by your place and had some tea, but your lights were out. It's all those Eskimo Pies. I'll try to make sure to drink more during the day so it doesn't happen again. You have a nice night, now."

With that, Bud hung up, locked the front door, turned out the lights, and went upstairs, ignoring the phone, which was again ringing.

Bud got into his Scooby Doo jammies and settled back in bed with one of Junior's Zane Grey books, "To the Last Man." It was nice to kick back and relax, he thought. Besides, he had a bit of a stomach ache.

He opened the book, then decided to go get some Tums from his overnight pack. The phone was again ringing, but he had no intention of answering it, as he didn't want to talk to Indie. But it just rang and rang, so he finally began wondering if maybe it were Junior or something important.

"Yell-ow."

"Bud, is Junior there?"

It was LuAnn.

"LuAnn! Is everything OK?"

"No, it's not. I need to talk to Junior."

"He's still gone. Is it something I can help with?"

"No. He's still off with Indie?"

"No, LuAnn, she only gave him a ride to the train. I haven't heard from him since."

"He really went through with it?"

"It appears so. Nobody's heard a word since, though Tom Turner got a collect call from some jail, but he didn't take it."

"Oh my god! He's in jail?"

"We're not sure it was him."

"So, the Mayor of Paradox is in jail. Serves him right. Where is he?"

"Nobody knows, LuAnn."

"I wish I knew so I could go pay him a little visit."

"I'm sure he would be glad to see you. When are you coming back?"

"Never," LuAnn snapped, hanging up the phone.

Bud shook his head, ate some Tums, and went back to his book, just as the phone began ringing again. Thinking it was LuAnn, he answered it.

"Yell-ow."

"Bud, you have to come over right now. There's someone lurking around the ranch. They're over at Annie's right now, but they were walking around outside my house. I'm scared to death. Please, Bud, hurry."

It was Indie.

CHAPTER 26

Bud pulled on his boots and cowboy hat and grabbed his jacket, after first quickly pulling his gun holster over his shoulder. He loaded his Ruger, then was on his way to Indie's in a flash.

It didn't take long to get there, but instead of parking at Indie's house, he cut his lights and pulled over along the road before getting to the big gate. He quietly got out and stealthily crept along the road next to the bushes where he was less likely to be seen.

He was soon at Indie's, and he could see she had all the lights in the house on, including the outside ones. It was easy to see the yard and even on out into the fields a bit, where several bats flew erratically around in their search for insects.

Bud paused and just watched for awhile. He could hear the spray of the big irrigation sprinklers hitting the nearby fields, a light on the end of each one signaling to Bodie that it was working.

As he stood in the shadows, leaning against a fence post, he thought of Annie. Was this late-night visitor why she didn't want to come back to the ranch? Were they now looking for her, and had they also been the ones responsible for Mack's murder?

Suddenly, Bud saw something move in the shadows over by Annie's house. He watched as someone crept around the perimeter of the house, trying to look in each window. Didn't they realize there was no one there?

Bud took his gun from its holster and put it in his jacket pocket, safety now off, where he could easily keep his hand on it. His other hand was now engaged in twirling the end of his mustache.

Now the figure disappeared around the corner of the house. Bud turned back to Indie's, and he could see her shadow, pacing back and forth. He knew she must be calling him again at the store, but he had no way of telling her he was on it and just outside her back porch, not without revealing himself to the stranger, anyway.

Soon, he heard the front door slam and a car start and saw Indie's Honda headed out to the main road. Good, he thought, she's smart to flee and get out of here, and it left him one less thing to worry about. On the other hand, it left him here all alone, which he didn't like.

He wondered if she would see his FJ parked in the shadows along the road and come back, but instead, she turned and went the other direction.

After a few minutes, he saw her turn at the Turner's house. This made him feel better, as she would be safe there, but he hoped Tom Turner wouldn't come over and get involved, as he would probably just put himself in danger.

Just then, he saw the shadowy figure come back around the house. He watched as it opened a window and climbed through. He should've used the key under the mat, Bud thought.

Bud's left leg was going to sleep, so he changed positions. He was tired, and he had no idea what to do at this point. He could call the sheriff, but he himself kind of was the sheriff, so that would do no good, and the real sheriff was a couple of hours away. He was pretty much on his own.

A chill came over him as he remembered what he'd seen at Junior's store the first evening he'd been here, and he now had to fight a sudden urge to flee. His Ruger would be useless if it were the wild man and it came after him.

Indie was now safe, so why was he staying and putting himself at risk? Personal safety was the number one rule of law enforcement, because if you weren't watching out for yourself, you sure couldn't watch out for anyone else.

But he needed to find out what was going on. This case was the most baffling thing he'd ever seen to date, and he had almost no leads—or maybe too many leads. And it seemed like everyone had a limp, just like whoever had dumped Mack's body.

Anyone could've murdered Mack, and so far everyone was a suspect, with a few exceptions, like Junior and Lu-Ann. But it could have easily been Tom, Bodie, Annie, or Indie who had murdered him, and all had their own motives. Or it could've been the wild man, who Bud suspected was the one now in Annie's house, no doubt looking for her. She had been smart to stay away, he could now see that.

Now something new caught Bud's eye—one of the irrigation lights had gone out! He knew they were connected to an alarm in Bodie's house.

Sure enough, he soon saw a figure walking across the fields from the direction of Bodie's place. Bud wanted to warn him, but had no way. He thought of firing a warning shot and then running for his FJ, but he knew he couldn't outrun the wild man, so he just stayed put and watched, hoping Bodie and the wild man wouldn't see each other.

He could see Bodie fiddling with the sprinkler, and at the same time, the figure climbed back out the window and began to walk around to the side of the house that Bodie was nearest.

Bud decided he might be wise to get a bit closer, in case Bodie needed his help, though he wasn't sure what he could do, so he silently slipped along the tree line down to the house.

Bud could see that the sprinkler light was now back on, and he sighed, hoping Bodie would now go away. Instead, Bodie tromped through the field and on over to the house, where he sat down on the front porch and appeared to be fiddling with his irrigation boots.

The figure crept around the corner and suddenly stopped, seeing Bodie.

Bud pulled the gun from his pocket, ready to use it but hoping not to.

Just then a motion sensor light came on, lighting up the entire front of the house. Bodie saw the now lit-up figure and jumped up.

"What the hell?" Bud heard him say.

The figure replied, "I'm looking for someone, and I bet you know where she is. She has something that belongs to me, and I want it back now."

It was Boonie.

Bud sighed and put the gun back into its holster. He had the feeling that he was about to add another person to his suspect list.

CHAPTER 27

Bodie stood up and looked at Boonie, saying, "You know you're 86'd from the ranch, Boonie. I'm supposed to call the sheriff if you show up here."

"Where's Annie? I only want to talk to Annie," Boonie replied.

"I don't know where she is. She never came back after Mack was killed."

"You have to know where she is. You work for her."

"I wish I did know, as I need to get paid. Boonie, you need to get out of here now. If Indie sees you here, she'll call the law. What the hell, coming around here this late to talk to Annie?"

"OK, OK, I'm leaving. But when you see Annie, tell her Boonie knows what she did, and it was way wrong. I'll catch up with her, and then she'll have some fast talking to do. And I want my stuff back."

"Are you threatening Annie?" Bodie was now clenching his hands into fists.

"I'm gone."

With that, Boonie turned and trotted back down the lane. Soon, Bud heard the sound of his old pickup sputtering down the road. He knew Boonie would soon see his FJ, but like Indie, Boonie turned and went the other direction.

For a moment, Bud wrestled with the thought of asking Bodie what was going on, but he was tired, so he just stood there silently in the shadows. Before long, Bodie headed back across the fields towards his own place.

Bud walked back to his FJ and got in, then decided to drive over to the Turner's to tell Indie it was safe to come home. He was again wishing the valley had cell phone coverage.

Bud rang the cow bell. Tom answered the door, looking hesitant until he saw who it was.

"Bud! What are you doing out so late?"

Bud answered, "I was just driving around the neighborhood looking for trouble. Indie here?"

"She is. Seems something strange is going on over at her place. Come on in."

"I can't stay," Bud answered, just as Indie came out from the kitchen with Susie. They were each holding a glass of wine.

"Indie," Bud said, "I scouted out your place and it's safe to go back now."

Indie looked suspicious. "How do you know that for sure?"

"It was Bodie fixing the irrigation system."

"Bodie? Why would he be walking around outside my house?"

"Things kind of got away from him. But it's safe now."

Indie hesitated, then said, "Well, OK, I'll head back over pretty soon. Me and Susie are having a nice discussion about things. Since she's an earth sign, I'm helping her with her house—she needs something yellow in the middle of the room here to meditate on. But she's a Taurus, and Tom's an Aquarius, and I'm explaining how those two signs can rarely communicate with each other, and they maybe need to have their auras balanced after so long together in disharmony."

Tom winked at Susie. "We've been through 30 years of successful non-communication."

"Well, that's interesting," Bud replied, "But I'm gonna go home and go back to bed."

As they walked to the door, Tom said, "Say, Bud, it's nice to know I'm not the only natty dresser in the valley." He grinned and pointed to Bud's Scooby Doo pajamas, the bottoms tucked into Bud's boots.

"All the latest rage outside the valley here," Bud mumbled. "Everyone in Green River has a pair. We wear 'em everywhere."

Bud stumbled down the long set of stairs and got into his vehicle as Tom stood on the landing, watching the FJ's taillights fade into the inky darkness of the Paradox Valley.

• • •

The next morning, Bud had just sat down to a breakfast of half-burnt toast and an overcooked egg when the phone rang. He was beginning to feel like he spent way more time on the phone here, where there was limited service, then he ever did where he had good cell service.

"Yell-ow," he answered.

"Say, is this Sheriff Bud Shumway I'm speaking to?"

It was Howie.

"Nope, this is Bud Shumway, but not Sheriff Bud Shumway." Bud paused, then added, "Well, wait a minute, maybe I am Sheriff Bud Shumway after all, Howie, since they hired me on here part-time, but I guess that would be Deputy Sheriff Bud Shumway."

"Don't confuse me, Sheriff," Howie replied. "You're hired on there part-time?"

"Yeah, there's been a little trouble, and the real sheriff is about three hours away, cause Paradox is in the far end of Montrose County, so they have an agreement with the San Miguel County Sheriff over in Telluride to cover for them, since he's only about two hours away, and he's asked me to cover for him, since I'm right here, even though I'm visiting from Green River, which is about four hours away."

"Geez Louise, Bud, that's even more confusing."

"Yeah, it is. What's up, Howie?"

"Well, this is about business, I mean real business, not band business, even though I know talking to you about band business would still be real business, since you're our band manager and all, but I mean, this is about sheriff's business."

Bud waited patiently.

Howie continued, "See, last night I got a call from the jailer over in Castle Dale. This is why they want to move the sheriff's office over there, cause it's so far away, the jail, that is, well, I guess the jailer, too. Anyway, he said one of the deputies up in Price picked up a hobo over by Cedar Siding, there on the railroad, and that's in our region, so they brought him to our jail."

"A hobo? Why did they pick him up?"

"He was riding in the caboose, drinking beer, and when the railroad guys found him, they tried to kick him off. It was at Cedar Siding, cause that's where they'd stopped and noticed him. But he wouldn't get off. He said it was too remote and he'd die out there, and he was probably right. So they had a deputy come down and arrest him."

Good lord, Bud thought, Cedar Siding was out in the middle of nowhere, just below Horse Bench and a good 20 or 30 miles from Price and Green River both. There truly was nothing there, except saltbush, creosote, and gnats— and an old road going down to the siding itself. Good thing the fellow had refused to get off there.

"So, what's the question here, Howie?" A lightbulb was beginning to go off in Bud's mind, though it was still kind of dim and flickering.

"Well, Sheriff, the question is, what do I do with this guy? Apparently he called a few places last night trying to find someone who would come bail him out, but had no luck. We can't afford to feed him for very long on our budget."

Bud thought for a minute, then said, "Howie, here's my advice. I say throw the book at him. Charge him with everything you can possibly come up with—vagrancy, trespassing, drinking in the vicinity of churches and schools, cause you know that train goes by both, whatever. All those fines will help your budget, plus he needs to learn a lesson about bumming off others."

"Gee, Bud, he's just some harmless old hobo. It didn't hurt the train any to give him a free ride."

"Doesn't matter, Howie, he needs to learn a lesson. You know, those old hobo ways were dying out, and it was a good thing, too. We don't want to see them make a comeback. You ever see some of the hobo signs they'd make around town? Innocent old ladies with hobo signs marked on their gateposts telling the world that they bake good apple pies and will give you a slice. It ran many of them to ruin, feeding hobos. We need to nip this in the bud. If word gets out that Emery County is good to hobos, you're gonna see a bunch of them hanging around Green River. Is that what you want?"

"Gee, Sheriff, I dunno. Would they ever buy a sandwich or two from Howie's Drive-In you suppose?"

"Howie, they'd be over there clogging up that drive-through window, begging."

"Well, gee, Sheriff..."

"You listen to what I say, Howie, you know I'm right. That old hobo guy will just have to learn the hard way. Was his name Junior, by any chance?"

"No, not Junior, it was something like Angus Fergus McSomething or O'Something or other, can't remember exactly."

"Is he Irish?" Bud asked.

"I dunno, Sheriff, I didn't drive over there to see him. It's too far."

"Well, I bet he's Irish. Riding in the caboose drinking beer sounds Irish to me."

"Aren't you part Irish, Bud?"

"Yes, I am, and that qualifies me to know about them, and Irish hobos are bad news, some of the worst. You better listen to me, Howie."

"Oh, I am, Sheriff, I am, believe me. Well, I guess I better go see what the book says about what charges I can file. Thanks for the advice, Sheriff."

"You're welcome, Howie, anytime."

Bud hung up, glad to finally know where his uncle was.

He went back into the kitchen and sat back down to his now-cold breakfast, thinking. He knew that Judge Richter over in Castle Dale would drop any and all charges Howie could come up with once he found out Junior had been riding the rails, as the judge was one of the biggest railroad fans on earth.

The judge was on the Board of Directors at the Helper Railroad Museum and also had an HO train setup in his garage that would be the envy of some real railroads. He often stopped in to say hello when Bud was sheriff in Green River, as he would come down just to watch the trains.

Bud knew the judge would not only drop the charges, but would take Junior out to lunch at the golf-course restaurant up in Helper, then to tour the museum. He'd probably even ask for his autograph.

Bud also knew that Junior didn't know that and would stew in jail for a couple of days until he came up in front of Richter, maybe thereby regretting riding the rails and vowing to never do it again.

In Bud's mind, this would be a goal worthy of the bit of subterfuge in which he'd just engaged.

CHAPTER 28

Bud went downstairs and opened the store. He noticed several notes on the counter, all from people who'd come in while he was gone yesterday and bought stuff. They were all charges. At this rate, the store would soon be empty, as Bud had no idea how to restock things. He hoped Junior would return before that happened.

Bud put up the sign, "Pay at Cafe," though he had no idea why, since the cafe was closed. He guessed it was to tell people nobody was around. He wondered if Junior ever had things stolen, but he knew he didn't, as the only ones who ever came into the store were from the valley.

Things sure had changed since he arrived, Bud thought as he closed the door and put on his hat, and not necessarily for the better. Everything seemed to be falling apart, and he had no explanations for anything. He wondered why LuAnn had called and if she were OK, though he suspected she was just calling to check up on Junior.

As he got in his FJ, he suddenly felt a wave of homesickness hit him—he wanted to see Wilma Jean and the pups, have a nice lunch of left-over meatloaf there in their country kitchen, then go out and mow the grassy lawn under the big globe willow and catalpa trees.

He sure had got himself into something more than he'd expected, he thought as he pulled up in front of the old hot springs. He saw a curtain pull back, then Annie standing in the open door, Maggie at her side.

"Morning, Annie. I have the checkbook."

Annie took it from Bud and started making out a check.

"How much should I make it for?" she asked.

"I dunno, how long's it been since Bodie was paid?"

"I don't have any idea. Mack always handled this kind of stuff."

"Well, how about making it for a month, then I can give it to him and ask how far behind you are. And while you're at it, why not pay off his grocery bill—$789.21. Make it out to Junior, then you can deduct that from Bodie's future pay-checks."

"Oh my gosh. He's that far behind?"

"A man's gotta eat. Good thing my uncle carries every-one, or this whole valley would be starved to death by now. But Junior has bills to pay, too."

"Oh, I know, I know."

Annie made out two checks and handed them to Bud, who put them in his pocket. He then pulled out the receipt from the state prison and showed it to her.

"Any idea what this is for?"

Annie turned white as a sheet. "No."

"It was on Mack's desk. By the way, Boonie showed up at your house last night. He was looking for you."

"I knew he would," Annie sounded panicked. "That's why I'm here and not there. You didn't tell him where I am, did you?"

"No. What's going on here, Annie?"

"I can't tell you."

"Why not?"

"It's self-incriminating. I can't tell you."

"Is it something you did?"

"Yes, but I can't tell you."

"Was it illegal?"

"Yes."

"Did it involve Boonie?"

"Yes."

"Did Boonie do something illegal?"

She paused. "No, not that I know of, anyway."

Bud replied. "And you wouldn't tell me if he had, right? You sound like a broken record. Just tell me and get it over with. Did you kill Mack?"

Annie turned even whiter than before. "No. Absolutely not."

"Did Boonie?"

She paused for a long time. "I don't know. It's possible, but I don't know."

Bud handed her a piece of paper. "Sign this. It's for the funeral home, authorizing them to cremate Mack's remains. I'm sorry, Annie."

She started crying as she signed the paper, then began to full-on sob. Bud put his arm around her, trying to comfort her. He noticed she had the faint odor of the plateau—of cedar and smoke and sagebrush.

"Annie, go on home. You can take a shower, get some clean clothes, try to process all this and make plans for the future. You can't stay holed up here. I can deal with Boonie. Indie will be there, you won't be alone. Bodie will keep an eye out, too."

"Bodie? He's part of the problem," Annie said, pulling back from Bud. "He's the reason all this happened."

"How so?" Bud asked hopefully, knowing full well her answer.

"I can't tell you."

"Can you tell me why you're limping?"

"One of the horses stepped on my foot."

"Was that when you were fleeing the ranch? Trying to get away from Mack?"

Annie frowned. "How did you know that?"

"Just a guess," he replied.

Bud turned to leave, then got something out of his FJ and turned back.

"Here, a little something for Maggie."

He handed Annie a box of "Rowdy Dog Biscuits, Wonderfully Tasty and Endorsed by Scooby Doo." His dogs loved them.

Annie smiled. "Thanks. Maggie loves these."

"OK, call me when you're ready to go home, Annie. Even though some of the evidence points to you, I know you didn't kill Mack. I don't know what you did that was so illegal, but I know it's a problem that's fixable."

"Thank you," Annie said, wiping her eyes.

Bud got into the FJ and backed out of the drive. He glanced over where Annie and Maggie had been, but they were gone, back inside the dusty decrepit old motel.

A mockingbird sat on the old sign, as if to mock Bud for thinking Annie would tell him anything. He wasn't positive Annie hadn't had anything to do with Mack's death, but he was sure at this point that she hadn't killed him herself.

He headed back to the store, just in time to be nearly sideswiped by an older beat-up brown van coming around a curve too fast, which slammed on its brakes and then began to fishtail, but managed to come to a stop.

"Hey, Mr. Shumway!" an excited voice called out. "Guess what we found! Gold! We're rich!"

It was Jimmy and Carl.

CHAPTER 29

Bud stopped his FJ and got out as Carl pulled the heavy side door of the van open.

"Woila!" Jimmy said, pointing to the same large pan they'd had the trout in, except now it held a big chunk of a golden-colored rock.

"Where'd you find this?" Bud asked, examining the chunk without picking it up.

"Can't tell you," Carl answered.

"I guess I can't tell you neither," echoed Jimmy.

Bud whistled, then leaned against the van, shading his eyes with one hand while twirling his mustache with the other.

"So, you boys think you found gold, huh? Are you gonna go over to the county seat in Montrose and stake a claim, assuming you found it on public lands..."

Jimmy's face now showed concern. "We have to stake a claim?"

Bud replied, "Well, unless it was on private land. But if you want to protect your interests, yes, you need to go stake a claim."

"What do we need to do to stake a claim?" Carl asked.

"I'm not sure what the procedure is these days, but

back when I was doing a little uranium prospecting, you had to mark the center and the corners of the claim with rock cairns and measure it all up, then go in and fill out the required paperwork."

"Does it cost anything?" asked Jimmy.

"Yes, if I recall, there was a fee, maybe a couple hundred dollars."

"What? Who has that kind of money?" Jimmy moaned.

"How do you know you were on public land?" Bud asked.

Carl pulled an atlas out from under the seat and opened it, then pointed to a color-coded map of Colorado.

"See, this brown stuff is BLM lands," he replied. "That's how we know."

"Well, that's not a very accurate map," Bud answered, "But it really doesn't matter, because that's not gold."

Both Jimmy and Carl looked shocked.

Bud continued. "It's carnotite. Uranium ore."

"Oh man, Mr. Shumway, isn't uranium really valuable, too?" Jimmy asked hopefully.

"It can be, but it's pretty volatile, and I don't just mean radioactively, which it is, but economically. The price floats a lot. No idea what it's worth these days."

Bud got back into his FJ, his arm hanging out the open window.

"Good luck, boys. Uranium mining is a big financial operation—I know, I used to be a miner. You're going to need an investor with a lot more cash than a lowly melon farmer like me has."

"Wait, Mr. Shumway!" Jimmy replied. "If we were to take you to where we found this, could you help us figure out if it's on public land so we can go file a claim?"

Bud paused. He really wasn't interested in having anything to do with prospecting or mining again, but his natural curiosity made him want to know where the carnotite came from.

"OK," he replied. "As long as it doesn't take all day to get there. I have a store to mind, mind you."

"Follow us," Carl said as he and Jimmy jumped into the van, gunning it so the tires spit rocks everywhere.

Bud followed along, and it wasn't long until the van turned onto the road he'd just come from, the one that led to the old hot springs. Bud was surprised, as he'd expected a drive up onto the flanks of the plateau, where the Morrison Formation was, the source of most of the uranium in this area.

But suddenly, the van veered onto the shoulder of the road and stopped. Bud pulled in behind it as Jimmy jumped out and came back to talk to him.

"I'm sorry, Mr. Shumway, but Carl's being all paranoid and thinks we need to think about this some more before we show anyone where it is. So I guess we're going to head on home to Naturita and come back tomorrow. We'll come by the store, assuming he changes his mind. I hope he does, cause we sure could use some help in the knowledge department. He also says we probably should tell Mr. Turner before we do anything, since he's grubstaking us."

"Tom Turner's grubstaking you to look for gold in the Paradox Valley?"

"No, not in the valley, up on the plateau. We're pretty much convinced there's gold up there, cause we found this—but don't tell nobody." Jimmy pulled a small piece of glittery rock from his shirt pocket and handed it to Bud.

Bud just shook his head. It was a piece of fool's gold—a nice piece, but still fool's gold. Iron pyrite.

Jimmy took the rock back and put it in his pocket, then continued. "But since we didn't find this carnotite stuff up there, it's kind of not part of the agreement with Turner, and I told Carl that, but I think he's thinking maybe Turner could still be an investor. We're beginning to realize that it takes money to make money, as they say."

"It's OK, Jimmy. You guys come back if you want, but do me a favor and don't sleep in your van with that rock tonight. It is radioactive, you know."

Jimmy reassured Bud they wouldn't, then hopped back into the van and the pair was gone.

Bud sighed. Turner grubstaking those two to look for gold in one of the least likely places around? That would explain Tom's comment on the phone to Junior about Paradox being set to have a big gold rush and hornet's nests being inevitable. It seemed to Bud that Carl and Jimmy were a big hornet's nest all on their own.

He knew that this could be tied in with Mack's murder, but he had no idea how, and he didn't want any more wild clues. He just wanted clues that made sense so he could solve the murder and go home.

But Bud now had a pretty good idea at this point of where the carnotite had come from, as the road they'd turned down dead-ended not far past the old hot springs at the old uranium mine. He was pretty sure he could find Jimmy and Carl's tracks, and he was also pretty sure they would lead right to the mine's tailings pile.

He turned around and headed back to the store. He needed to go check on things at there, and he also had a call to make, then maybe he'd come back and see what he could find.

CHAPTER 30

Bud hung up the phone and closed his eyes, trying to make sense out of the information he'd just received from the Utah State Prison in Draper.

He'd had to wait while they checked his credentials with the San Miguel Sheriff's office before they would release anything, but they'd finally called him back with the details of what Mack's big prison purchase had been.

It seems that the prison had a large greenhouse operation that used prisoners as employees, and their specialty was growing native plants for the State of Utah to use in reclamation projects, though they also sold retail to the public.

Mack had purchased over $2000 worth of native plants, including chokecherries, buffalo berry, sumac, Brigham tea, and cliffrose. All were hardy plants that would do well in the Paradox Valley, according to the prison, and at about 33 cents each for bare-root plants, the moving van Mack had used to pick them up was pretty much stuffed full.

When asked, the prison salesman said he remembered Mack, as it was unusual to sell that many plants to the public.

Bud tapped his fingers on the top of the counter holding the "King of the Road" lyrics. He wondered how Uncle Junior was doing in the jail over at Castle Dale, and if Howie had been able to throw the book at him.

Junior was probably having lunch with Judge Richter right now, Bud thought, the store's screen door slamming as he left. He had a stop to make, one that would take him out to Mack's ranch and that field Bodie had thought might be drugs, and he dearly hoped Indie was gone.

As he pulled into the long lane, he relaxed, noting that Indie's car was indeed gone. Hopefully, she was in Telluride and wouldn't be coming back soon, as he wasn't sure where to begin his search.

A thought was starting to form in his mind, just an inkling of one, and he needed to check out his hunch. He pulled up in front of Mack and Annie's house and got out, then walked across the lane to where Annie's art studio sat on a small hill.

There, on that bit of a rise, he stood, slowly turning in a circle as he fiddled with his mustache, looking out into the fields. The big circular sprinklers were silent, and Bud guessed they were set to run only at night, helping conserve water by keeping it from evaporating in the heat of the day. There was no sign of Bodie anywhere.

Bud could see several green fields of what looked to be timothy hay, and next to those were the deeper rich greens of alfalfa. Over against the Turner fence was the buffalo field, which was starting to show signs of overgrazing with its browner color.

But there, next to the buffalo was a large field where the color and texture were different. It also bordered the Turner ranch, and though Bud couldn't make out what was growing in it, he thought he already knew.

He debated whether to walk to the field or be lazy and drive to the Turner's. Deciding it might be a good time to kill two birds with one stone and ask Tom about grubstaking Jimmy and Carl, he walked back to his FJ and steered it on back up the lane, taking a left and pulling up in front of the big log mansion with the cow bell.

Bud didn't see any vehicles around and nobody came to the door when he rang the bell, so he walked across the big lawn, almost tripping over the train tracks, then headed to the fence line that bordered the field he wanted to examine. He noted that the fence, unlike all the others on the ranch, was made of rustic wood.

As he pulled himself up onto the lower bar to see better, a huge flock of red-wing blackbirds startled and flew up, then settled back down in another part of the field. What looked to be a ground squirrel ducked into a hole as a rough-legged hawk's shadow drifted over it.

It was exactly as Bud had suspected—the entire field had been carefully filled with the native plants from the prison, small irrigation ditches running between each row.

Bud could see a few alfalfa plants here and there, their buds starting to purple up, and he knew Mack had taken a productive alfalfa field, one that stood to make him good money, and planted it with natives, which weren't even a crop. The question was, Why?

Now he noticed a sign about thirty feet down the fence line, shining in the direct sun, and he slipped down off the wooden fence and walked over to it.

It was one of three, the other two being next to it and not visible from where he'd been. They looked like the kinds of signs one would see in an interpretive center or national park. He started reading the first one:

"The Paradox Valley is a birder's paradise. You can spot a hundred or more species here in a good day in mid-May. The most species ever found in a year by the world's record-holding birder is less than 700, so one can see one-seventh of that record in one day here."

Bud moved over to the next sign.

"As one moves from the valley and up onto the Un-compahgre Plateau, you can typically see seven species of woodpeckers, nine species of flycatchers, eight jay species, six swallow species, eight chickadee species, eight creepers species, five wrens and dippers species, five thrushes species, seven to ten warbler species, and a dozen sparrow species."

He moved to the third sign.

"Other birds often seen include the black-chinned hummingbird, gray flycatcher, ash-throated flycatcher, plumbeous vireo, Bewick's wren, black-throated gray warbler, spotted towhee, gray catbird, indigo bunting, yellow-breasted chat, canyon and rock wrens, white-throated swift, gambel's quail, marsh wren, gray catbird, Bullock's oriole, chimney swift, northern waterthrush, peregrine falcon, white-throated swift, broad-tailed hummingbird, flycatchers, American three-toed woodpecker, northern saw-whet owl, gray jay, and red-breasted nuthatch. This is only a partial list."

The signs were facing the Turner ranch, and Bud wondered what in the heck was going on. Why would Mack replant a large productive alfalfa field, pay good money to build a nice wooden fence around it, put in native plants, and then put up these signs, which had to be expensive to make? It just didn't make sense.

It had to be part of the Wild West theme park, Bud postulated, but a sort of a concession to Annie, who didn't want to see the valley developed and who also loved birds and animals. That had to be it. If the Turner's house was going to be the headquarters, the signs were pointed in the right direction for people to come from there and see the bird field.

Bud turned and walked back over the Turner's lawn and got into his FJ. He then decided it was time to go make himself something to eat. He was hungry enough that even a can of Dinty Moore stew from Junior's store sounded good.

But first, he wanted to search one last place on Mack's ranch, a place he and Joe hadn't known existed the first time they looked, a place he'd discovered from standing on the fence looking at the bird signs.

CHAPTER 31

Bud pulled onto a small road that led out to the buffalo herd, then parked as close to the field as he could get, almost up against the fence, noting that the animals were already aware of his presence and slowly ambling in his direction.

He hoped he could get to the small structure he'd seen from the bird field before the buffalo made it over his way.

He checked the fence, then ducked under the hotwire and began running to what looked like a springhouse in the corner where the buffalo field met the bird field.

He knew he probably should've gone the long way, but it meant walking all the way through the bird field, and he was tired. He hoped he hadn't underestimated the buffalos' speed and curiosity.

Looking over his shoulder, he could now see the buffalo picking up their pace, coming directly towards him. They wanted to see what was going on, and Bud knew they could be dangerous if they felt threatened. He hoped the door was unlocked to the small building that sat by the irrigation head gate.

For some reason, it looked to him like the perfect place to hide something, and he and Joe hadn't searched it, as it wasn't visible from the main ranch buildings.

What would be hidden there, he had no idea, but he wanted to be thorough. Besides, he needed all the clues he could get on this case, it was a tough one and he didn't feel like he was making any progress at all.

The herd was now running directly towards him, and he realized he had indeed underestimated their curiosity and speed, as well as their territoriality.

Bud was now running as fast as he could, and he sure hoped that little springhouse or whatever it was was unlocked.

He arrived just in time, jerking the door open and almost tumbling inside as the buffalo stampeded right up to the door. For a moment, he was afraid they would come right on through the building, which was small enough that a buffalo could probably knock it over if it hit it.

He stood in the dark, huffing and puffing, trying to be as quiet as possible as several buffalo snorted and rubbed up against the building. He felt humbled, hoping nobody had seen his stupidity on full display just now. He should've gone the long way through the bird field.

Finally, the buffalo seemed to lose interest, and he could hear them wandering away. He opened the door a crack—it was all clear. He now had enough light to see what was inside the building, but he wasn't sure what to make of it.

Leaning against one wall were some irrigation tools—shovels and tarps, but against the other wall were a dozen or more animal traps of various sizes, as well as two guns. The traps looked vicious, and a few were large and looked to be bear traps. He inspected the guns—one was a shotgun and the other a .22 caliber rifle. Both looked well-used and old, as did the traps.

Bud wasn't sure what to make of all this. Was Mack a trapper and hunter and had hidden his stuff here so Annie wouldn't know? Had she found out and murdered him? It didn't seem likely that a gentle animal lover would murder a human for killing animals, but he'd heard of stranger things, real paradoxes.

Or did it all have something to do with Bodie? Annie had claimed that Bodie was the one to blame for all this, so maybe he'd been trapping animals here on the ranch and this somehow triggered a series of events that had led to Mack being killed.

In any case, he knew he'd found some kind of clue, but he had no idea what it meant or how to decipher it.

He now cracked open the door a bit further, looking to see if any of the buffalo had come back. They were now over by his FJ, and he hoped he hadn't parked it close enough to the fence for them to chew on it.

There was no way Bud could get back to his FJ without the buffalo seeing him, so he decided to duck under the fence and walk back through the bird field. It was a long walk, but at least it was safe—though muddy.

The ditches were running and he had no choice but to walk right down them, as the rows of plants were too tight to walk through. Whoever had planted the field had placed the native plants so they would grow into a jungle, a perfect habitat for birds and critters.

As he sloughed along, his Herman Survivor boots not as waterproof as the ads had claimed, Bud thought of the traps. It really was a paradox—animal traps in the middle of an animal sanctuary. He really couldn't figure that one out.

Nor could he figure out what a small green nylon tent was doing in the middle of the field, so well hidden he'd just about tripped over it. He stopped and turned around to examine it closer.

Someone had pulled up a small area of plants, making just enough room to pitch a small tent in the middle of the row where it wouldn't get wet from the irrigation water. It was a perfect hiding place, as one couldn't see it until you were right on it.

Bud stood over the tent, noting the door was zipped up, then finally said, "Anybody in there?"

He was hoping the answer would be "no" and was unprepared when a deep growly voice answered instead, "Go away."

CHAPTER 32

Bud wasn't sure what to do. It appeared that someone was living in the middle of Annie's field, but he couldn't understand why. It was another paradox—why would someone pitch a tent here instead of somewhere on nearby public lands, where nobody cared if they camped or not? And who was inside the tent?

He pulled his Ruger from its shoulder holster and put it in his pocket, safety off. He didn't like the sound of that voice one bit, but as deputy sheriff, he was obligated to investigate. It was clearly a case of trespassing.

"I'm Deputy Sheriff Bud Shumway, and I think you might want to come on out so we can talk about your choice of a camp spot. I can help you find something a little better, where you're not trespassing, if you'll let me."

Bud sure didn't want to further antagonize whoever was in there, as he already sounded mad—and maybe big.

The zipper was now unzipping, and Bud stood back a bit, but was unprepared for what emerged from the small tent. He wondered how in hellsbells the guy could even fit in there. He must sleep on his back and never move, Bud thought.

A very large man emerged, having a bit of trouble pulling himself up through the small door without pulling the whole tent down around him. He was older, maybe in his 70s, Bud guessed from all his gray hair, and there was plenty of it, as it hung down onto his shoulders in a tangled mass. He wore faded sweat pants and a torn and dirty plaid shirt and no shoes. His feet were huge, and Bud guessed that's why he didn't wear shoes—he probably couldn't find anything that fit.

Now the man stood up, towering a good foot over Bud, who felt more than a little intimidated. He knew he was face to face with the person who had conked Junior on the head, but he had no intention of trying to arrest him. Just like that night he'd seen him escaping from the back of Junior's store.

Bud knew now it was the wild man, right here in Annie's field, not up on the plateau where he was supposed to be.

"Nice meeting you," Bud held out his hand, against his better judgement. To his surprise, the man held his out and shook with him. His handshake was nothing like Bud expected—instead of tearing his hand off, it was limpid and gentle.

"Likewise," said the wild man in his deep gravelly voice.

"Say, I didn't get your name," Bud replied.

"Jerry. My name's Jerry Stover."

"What the heck are you doing living out here, Jerry? Don't you get your feet wet when Bodie's irrigating?"

Jerry replied, "I'm here with permission. Mack said I could stay here. I work for him."

Bud paused. If the wild man had killed Mack, he was doing a good job of acting innocent, like he didn't even know Mack was dead.

"What kind of work?" Bud asked.

"Whatever he needs. I do the stuff nobody else will do. "

"Like conk people over the head when they won't sell out?"

Bud couldn't believe he had just said that—like running through the buffalo field, he figured he must still be feeling suicidal.

But instead of getting mad, the wild man hung his head.

"I really didn't mean to hit him—he scared me and I overreacted."

"My Uncle Junior scared a big guy like you? But what were you doing there in his store, if you weren't hired by Mack to intimidate Junior?"

"I was hungry and was going to beg groceries. Mack and Annie were gone, so I couldn't ask them, and Bodie had told me not to come over to his place, as he didn't want anyone to know he knew I was here. I went to the back of the store where Junior was and saw he had a gun, and I panicked, but I realized after I hit him that it was a pricing gun, the kind that makes stickers. It wouldn't be the first time someone's shot at me, so I'm kind of gun shy. Then someone came in so I hid, then ran."

"No need to beg for food. Junior lets everyone buy on credit. No need to whack people, either."

"I been living in the wilds too long." Jerry replied. "I'll work at his store or whatever he needs doing, just don't arrest me. Being in jail would kill me off."

"Well, we'll have to consult with Junior on that, and he's currently out of town. But what do you usually eat out here?" Bud wondered if the traps and guns were the wild man's.

"Mack usually brings me food. No idea why he stopped. He puts it over in the weeds. I work it off by irrigating this field. It's Annie's field, you know, Mack did it for Annie. She loves birds. But it's a big secret. He wants to surprise her with it."

"I thought you were prospecting up on the plateau."

"I was, but it got too hairy up there for me."

"Hairy?"

"Yeah, there's a weird creature up there, a Bigfoot or something. I was feeding it, but it finally scared me off. I'm never going back."

Bud whistled. "You were feeding it? You're braver than I am. I know all about that guy. He paid me a visit at the Ute Tower—unless that was you."

"Wasn't me. I'm too old and stoved up to climb all those stairs. But the plateau's a big waste of time. There's no gold up there anyway, and I knew that. Just another of my insane boondoggles."

"Do you know some kids named Carl and Jimmy?"

"I do, yes, they came up a few times when I was up there, trying to get me to help them find gold. They're a bit off, if you know what I mean, the kind of fellows who don't want to work for a living."

Bud found that statement a bit ironic, paradoxical, even.

As if he could read Bud's thoughts, the wild man replied, "And I have to agree with them in some ways. Working for wages is pure slavery—I prefer to do trades and stuff, like for Mack here, me helping him out and him helping me out."

Now Bud wasn't sure what to do. Should he tell Jerry his snack wagon was gone, that Mack was dead? The old guy acted like he really didn't know, which made him less of a suspect, unless it was an act. Bud suddenly felt sorry for him, nothing to eat and all stoved up like he was, barely able to get out of his tiny tent.

"Jerry, how did you end up down here, working for Mack? Does Annie know?"

"No, I doubt if she does, as she'd be scared to death of me like everybody else is. I stay away from the house, don't want her or that nutty Indiana gal seeing me. Boonie told me she's flakey as a butter roll. But I met Mack up on the plateau. He had Boonie working up there, doing some kind of weird thing up in the trees, a fake Ute burial, and I told Boonie to skeedaddle. He was in my territory, and when I found out what was going on, I shut it down.

"Then Mack came riding up one day to my little lean-to and brought me some real good whiskey, and we had a confabulation and came to an agreement that I would let him do his tourist thingy if he'd supply me with groceries and whiskey from there on out. I have a mining claim up there, all legal, and he was building this crap on my claim, these tree burials.

"But all of a sudden, he quit bringing me supplies. Boonie came by, and we sort of made up, and he told me Mack had done the same to him, sort of reneged on his deal. So I came down the hill and found Mack here on the ranch, and he said he'd decided not to do the tourist thingy after all, but I could stay and help him do this bird thing here in the field. So I did. I hand-planted this damn field, all by myself. But now it looks like Mack's reneged again."

"How long you been camping here?"

"A couple of months. I left for a bit when that damned Bigfoot came down here, messing around and stampeding the buffalo. I think it was looking for me, so I went over and hid by that old hot springs for a couple of days.

"It came back once a few days ago, but didn't stay. Scared me to death, howling and all, but couldn't find me. I think it was wondering where I'd gone to, as we were kind of buddies, at least in its mind—it would come around my place, and I'd throw it scraps. The way things are going, I'm about ready to go ride the rails again. Nobody cares if I starve to death or not, so I might as well die having fun."

Bud couldn't believe his ears. "You used to ride the rails?"

"Yup, for many years."

"My Uncle Junior, you know, the guy you conked over the head, he used to be a railroad hobo, too."

Jerry looked even more contrite. "You mean to tell me I whacked a fellow bum over the head? There's sure no pride in that."

"Say, you're a big guy. Were you down by the river throwing rocks at fish, and maybe even turned over a backhoe?"

"Throwing rocks at fish? Why would I do that? I ain't got nothin' against a bunch of poor fish. And I may be big, but I ain't big enough to budge no backhoe."

Bud wondered if maybe there weren't really a Bigfoot around, though he was inclined to not believe in them himself. But something had turned that backhoe over. It was a mystery, and one that probably would never be solved, as the wrecking company had come and pulled it from the river and taken it away for salvage.

Bud then grinned. He was kind of taking a liking to the wild man, proving Wilma Jean's theory that he liked everybody. But he still wasn't sure if he should tell him Mack was dead.

"Say, Jerry, you're in kind of a bind here. Tell you what, when I leave, I'll go back to the store and get you some supplies and bring them back. I'll put them over by the road behind that big sagebrush. Maybe that can tide you over until you get things figured out a bit."

Jerry looked relieved. "I can't tell you how much I would appreciate that. Maybe you could make a tab for me and put it on it."

"You know anything about some stuff in that spring-house over there?" Bud asked.

"No, nothing of mine, whatever it is. I'm too scared of them damn buffalo to mess around over there."

"Oh, it's nothing, just some junk. But say, can you tell me more about what happened when the Bigfoot or whatever it was came down here and you left for a couple of days?"

"Well, I could hear somebody arguing over at the main house—it sounded like Mack and Annie. Then doors slammed and I heard the horses all riled up and running around, then that ended, and I heard the Bigfoot howling and those damn buffalo stampeding, sounded like they broke out of their field. It all scared me to death, so I hightailed it over to Bodie's place, hid in the bushes, then hoofed it down the road as fast as I could go to the old hot springs and hid in the garage there for a couple of days."

"Was there anyone else around there?"

"Not at first, but after a couple of days, somebody came in and I left. No idea who it was, but I know that Bigfoot hung around awhile, cause I stopped down by the river to take a bath, and I saw its tracks."

"You then came straight back here?"

"I did, and I expected Mack to bring me some groceries, but that's when it stopped. I ended up borrowing some food from the Turners over there. I hated doing that, but I was about dead."

"You went inside?"

"Well, old Tom, he has a fridge over in his train garage where he keeps beer and snacks. I only borrowed a few things, and I'm planning on paying him back."

"Well, that borrowing's maybe not such a good idea. I sure wouldn't want to have to arrest you for stealing."

"I know, I know, but I was about dead. I sure wanted to take that train for a joyride, but I restrained myself."

"That's good. But look, I'm gonna go now, and I'll bring you some groceries in a couple of hours. But Jerry, you need to know that Mack didn't renege on his deal, he was murdered. And I'm going to maybe need your help figuring out who did it."

The look on Jerry's face told Bud all he needed to know.

The wild man was innocent.

CHAPTER 33

Bud had hiked back to where he'd left his FJ, relieved to see that the buffalo couldn't quite reach it over the hotwire. But they were still there, as if waiting for him, and one big bull was pawing the ground and looking at Bud like it would sure like to have him for lunch.

Bud was pretty sure buffalo were generally vegetarians, but he wasn't going to test his theory. As he got inside his vehicle, he felt a bit better, and it was then that he noticed the big bull had the tip of its horn broken off. Bud wondered whether he'd broken it off fighting another bull.

He put the FJ in reverse and turned around, then headed back down the road, stopping at the ranch house and getting out. He wanted to go inside and look for something—anything that might provide some clue as to what was going on. He really hadn't gone thoroughly through Mack's desk, and he was hoping something in the big stack of papers there might shine some light on things.

He got the key from beneath the front mat and opened the door. It was all just like when he'd been there last, except now it was daylight and not so lonely.

In Mack's office, he sat down at the big rolltop desk and began methodically going through the big stack of papers that threatened to spill off the desk. He wasn't sure what he was looking for, but he just felt like he needed to be thorough. He might find something that would shed some light on things, though he was doubtful.

This was one hodgepodge of papers, and it struck him that Mack must be one of these people who appear to be totally disorganized but who can find things via visual memory. He himself was kind of like that, and it drove Wilma Jean crazy.

Thinking of Wilma Jean, he thought maybe he would just give her a call, since Mack's phone was right here on his desk. He could call collect and not worry about anyone minding.

He dialed the operator, then asked to call the Melon Rind Cafe in Green River collect, as he figured Wilma Jean would be there at this time of day.

To his surprise, Howie answered.

"Melon Rind Cafe, Sheriff Howie speaking."

"I have a collect call from a Mr. Bud Shumway. Will you accept the charges?"

Bud wasn't sure he really wanted to talk to Howie collect, but it was too late, as Howie had already accepted the charges.

"Hey, Sheriff, is that really you calling collect? I hope Wilma Jean doesn't mind that I said it was OK."

"No, it's OK, Howie, she'll be alright with that. Is she there?"

"No, she and Maureen ran off to Price to do errands, leaving me to run things. It's my day off, and I know how to run a cafe, for sure—it's one of the few things I do know how to do. Say, I bet you're calling about our new gig over in Thompson Springs."

"Really? You have a gig? Are you ready for that?"

"Well, it's kind of not really a gig, since it's not paying anything, but we're going to play for a friend of Barry's who's having a birthday party. Won't be a lot of people there, so it should be a good way to do a test run on everything." Howie sounded enthusiastic.

Bud had already suspected there wouldn't be many people there, as the little town had maybe 100 people max.

"But hey, Sheriff, is everything OK over there? When you coming back? We need our band manager, now that we're ready to start playing for the public. Well, at least I think we are. I guess we'll know soon enough." Howie's enthusiasm sounded like it was already fizzling out.

Bud answered, "Well, when you get done there, maybe you can come over here and play. But how're things going in general? Wilma Jean doing OK?"

"She's fine, Sheriff. She and Maureen are cooking up a new menu for the cafe and they're getting supplies."

"What kind of menu?" Bud hoped it would still have his favorites on it, like the hot roast beef sandwich and the chicken fried steak. He wished he were there to have a say in it.

"They said Chinese."

Bud was shocked. A Chinese restaurant in Green River, home to melon farmers and cattle ranchers? It would sink just like that house that had tipped off the moving company truck last summer and landed right smack in the river.

"Chinese? Did you really say Chinese?"

"Well, Sheriff, I don't think it's a good idea, myself. But we'll just have to see what they come up with. I kind of like it like it is, and it seems to me if it ain't broke, don't fix it."

"I think you're right, Howie," Bud concurred. "Tell Wilma Jean I called, would you? Tell her I miss her and hope to be home soon."

"I will, Sheriff. You take care over there. Any progress on the murder?"

"Not really. It's a tough one, Howie. I just want to figure it out so I can come home."

"Well, we sure miss you over here. Say, I forgot to tell you one other thing."

Bud waited, but Howie was mum. Bud knew it was like using a crowbar to pry information out of Howie.

"What's that, Howie?" he finally asked.

"Glad you asked. Wilma Jean and Maureen are going over to visit that old hobo in the jail on their way home. I threw the book at him, just like you said to, and he's in big trouble, I can tell you that. So they get word of this, well, actually, I told them about it, and they decide to go pay the old guy a visit. Darndest thing I ever heard. They're sure a couple of bleeding hearts."

This news bothered Bud, as he knew Wilma Jean would recognize Junior and probably go his bail, which was not what he wanted. But there wasn't much he could do about it now. He sighed.

"Well, OK, I'm sure it will all work out. Anyway, I better go since this is collect and costing a fortune. Tell Wilma Jean I'll call again tomorrow from the store."

"OK, Sheriff. 10-4, over and out."

Bud hung up the phone and pondered the idea of Junior coming back. He guessed that would be OK, but he hoped his uncle never found out Bud's role in getting the book thrown at him. He thought about calling Wilma Jean collect and trying to head her off at the pass, but he wasn't sure you could make collect calls to a cell phone.

He now began going back through Mack's papers, and it wasn't long until he found something of interest—in fact, two things of interest. One was Mack's will, and the other appeared to be a contract of some kind. Bud grabbed both without looking at them—he wanted to go back to the store.

He walked out the door and locked it behind him, and as he was placing the key back under the mat he noticed something in the dirt not far from where he'd parked his FJ.

Bud picked it up and examined it. It was an off-white color, just like the piece of plastic he'd found up under the Ute tree burials—except it wasn't plastic, but was the real deal, some kind of bone.

He stood there thinking for a moment until it hit him— it had to be the missing tip of that buffalo bull's horn.

CHAPTER 34

Bud had just finished off a can of Dinty Moore beef stew from Junior's store and had leaned back from the table, wishing he had an Eskimo Pie, when a thought struck him.

If Annie had somehow been in cahoots with Bodie to kill Mack, why had she told Bud that Bodie was part of the problem and the reason everything had happened? She wouldn't want to incriminate her partner in crime, nor cast any kind of suspicion on him.

But Bodie easily could have been the man Bud saw in the shadows that night the backhoe dumped Mack's body in the river. He even had a limp, although it seemed everyone else did, too. Everyone but Indie, who instead had a spear.

Maybe Bodie had taken it upon himself to take care of Annie's problem without her knowledge. In any case, she knew something about Bodie that Bud didn't, and he needed to know what it was.

Bud now picked up the two documents he'd retrieved from Mack's desk and started looking them over. One was a contract, and it carefully outlined its terms in great detail. Bud wasn't real sure what he was reading, and it got pretty technical fast, so he picked up the second document, Mack's will.

As he read, it became very clear that Annie was indeed Mack's heir. Most of the property he'd already owned was already in her name and his, so there would be no probate to go through, it was already hers. This included a number of buildings in Telluride, as well as land in Montana, a golf course in California, and a house in Arizona. Mack also had some sizable bank accounts which all went to Annie. It appeared Annie was now very wealthy, which Bud had already guessed to be the case.

As he read the list of Mack's assets, Bud wasn't surprised to see that Mack had managed to acquire most of the Paradox Valley, with the exception of Junior's store and a couple of houses whose owners wouldn't sell. This made Annie kind of like a queen or something, he figured—the Queen of Paradox. The name kind of suited her, he thought.

But he then came to the other part of the will, and it now made the first document, the contract, clear—shockingly clear. Annie would get nothing in Paradox, not even the house or art studio she'd helped build.

It appeared that Annie owned everything Mack had acquired except the Paradox Valley. Indie would get the house and art studio, but no land other than a few acres around them.

Bud wasn't sure what to think. He grabbed some Tums, put on his holster and gun, made a phone call to the Montrose County coroner, then headed back downstairs and into Junior's supply room. It was time to get some of that Evolution Ale that Junior sold under the counter and go pay Boonie a visit.

Bud needed to know why Annie was hiding from Boonie and what she'd done to make Boonie so mad. Something had made Mack want her out of the valley, since he'd left the place to Indie—maybe it was Annie's own wishes, but maybe Mack was trying to protect her from something, and Bud suspected that something could very well be Boonie. Or maybe Mack was just mad at Annie for not cooperating and wanting to stay in Paradox with him.

Bud looked around a bit, but couldn't find any beer, so he instead grabbed a six-pack of orange soda and headed out, also sticking a couple of cigars in his pocket. Maybe that would pacify Boonie and get him to talk. He had already loaded up some groceries for the wild man and would swing by there on his way back.

Bud wasn't exactly sure how to find where Boonie lived, as all he knew was it was off the Divide Road. He'd written it down on a little piece of paper and stuck it in his wallet, and he pulled it out:

"County Rd 16, six miles off the Divide Road on the left."

It wasn't much for directions, Bud thought, as one could be going either direction down the Divide Road, wherever that was. If he knew which way the roads were numbered, it would help—east to west or west to east?

About all he knew was that the Divide Road ran along the crest of the plateau and there were several other roads that connected with it. He decided he would go on up the road he and Junior and Indie had driven down when he'd been rescued from the Ute Tower and see if that connected.

But first, he needed to get gas, and the nearest station was over in Naturita, some 25 miles away. He wasn't used to having to travel so far to fuel up and hoped he would make it, as the gas tank was now riding on empty.

He pulled out onto the road. He was soon at the turn-off to the old hot springs when a green Subaru pulled out, swerving and nearly hitting him, then hightailing it down the road. Right smack behind it was an old beat-up blue Dodge pickup with stock racks, and it appeared it was trying to run down the Subaru.

Bud suddenly realized Annie and Maggie were in the Subaru, and Boonie was chasing them! He quickly swung his FJ around, doing a U-turn right smack in the middle of the road, and joined the chase. He didn't have to worry about getting lost on the plateau any more, Bud thought, as Boonie was down here.

He had almost caught up to Boonie when all of a sudden the FJ started sputtering and the engine went dead—he'd run out of gas.

Bud coasted to the side of the road, kicking himself for waiting so long to refill his tank. He just hadn't wanted to drive all the way to Naturita until he was going that direction anyway. But the timing couldn't have been worse.

He got out. There was no way he could even call anyone. He locked the FJ and started walking back towards Junior's store, which he figured was about three miles away.

If he were lucky, he'd get there just in time to get a call from someone saying either Annie had fled the valley or had been shot by Boonie, was all he could figure. He could only hope for the former instead of the latter.

CHAPTER 35

Bud's Herman Survivors must've shrunk a bit from walking in the irrigation ditches, because he felt like he was getting blisters, and he hadn't been walking all that far. He knew he should've taken them off when he got back to Junior's and let them dry out, but he wasn't expecting to be hiking right away.

As he trudged down the road, he was passed by someone who suddenly came to a screeching stop, fishtailing and nearly running off the road, then backing up and nearly running over Bud, who jumped in the borrow ditch at the last moment.

It was Carl and Jimmy, and Bud had to admit to himself that he was actually happy to see them for once.

"Hey, Mr. Shumway, you need a ride? We saw your Toyota parked by the road back there. Did it break down?"

"Kind of—I guess you might say that," Bud answered as Jimmy opened the sliding side door.

"Where you wanna go?" Carl asked congenially. Bud suspected he was enjoying seeing a deputy sheriff on foot.

Bud thought for a moment. These two would know how to siphon gas, and he could thereby save having to ride with them all the way to Naturita and back, if he could only find a vehicle to siphon gas from—legally, of course. In fact, he suspected they would even somehow have a hose handy for the siphoning.

"Let's go to the general store. I need gas, and we can siphon some from Junior's pickup."

"Is that legal?" Jimmy asked innocently.

"Of course it is if you have permission," answered Bud.

"How can you have permission when he's gone?" Carl asked.

"It's a kind of standing permission," Bud replied, trying not to sound irritated.

They were soon at the store, where Bud rounded up an old gas can from the back, then watched as the pair deftly managed to siphon a couple of gallons from the tank of Junior's old truck.

"That should be enough to get me to Naturita, boys," Bud said, handing them each a cold orange soda from Junior's cooler.

They took him back to his FJ, where Bud poured the gas into the tank, got in, and started it up. He paused for a moment, the image of Boonie chasing Annie still in his mind, then did a quick calculation.

He got about 16 miles per gallon, and he figured they'd put about two and one-half gallons in the tank, so he could go about 40 miles before he ran out again. Naturita was only 25 miles, so that left him a good 15 miles extra, enough to cruise the valley once and see if he could spot Annie or Boonie.

He pulled out in the direction of the store, noting that Carl and Jimmy followed him. They were probably wondering why he was going the wrong way for gas, and he kind of hoped they continued to follow in case he ran out again. He hoped Junior's pickup had more gas in it.

Bud turned down the lane to Big Mack's Little Ponderosa Ranch, thinking maybe Annie had gone to Indie's for help, but there was nobody around, and even Indie's Honda was gone.

He turned around and drove back up the lane, passing Carl and Jimmy, who had turned and were now coming down the lane, following him. He nodded congenially at them as they passed, then watched in his rear-view mirror as they turned around and continued to follow.

Now Bud turned left on the main road, heading towards Turner's Rancho Not So Grande. When he got to their lane, he was surprised to see not only Annie's car parked in front of the house, but also Boonie's pickup and Indie's Honda.

Maggie sat in the Subaru, patiently waiting for Annie, her head hanging out the window as she watched the buffalo across the field.

Maybe the Turners were having a party, he thought, wondering if everyone was hanging out in the kitchen with Susie drinking wine and talking about grape varietals. For some reason, he thought it might be good for a deputy sheriff to stop in, as things could be getting pretty dramatic by now.

He pulled into the drive and parked next to Boonie's old truck, and Jimmy and Carl pulled in next to him.

"What's going on?" Jimmy asked. "Is it a party?"

"Maybe," Bud replied. "Come on in. You can be my guests."

At this point, Bud was thinking he could use all the reinforcements he could get, assuming the boys would take his side, which he knew could be a faulty assumption.

Bud rang the doorbell, and the cow mooed as Susie let them in. Just then, Bud heard gunshots from inside the house.

"Welcome to the party, everyone," Susie smiled graciously, ignoring the shots. "Come on in and have some wine and crackers. Boonie and Annie were ready to duke it out, but Tom's got them both diverted momentarily with his quick-draw act. He's really quite good. Don't be alarmed if you hear gunfire—it's just him shooting blanks. I'd rather he didn't shoot them off inside the house, but when he has an audience, there's no stopping him. And Indie's here, too."

Susie's smile then turned into a drawn look as she noted yet another guest coming up the drive, but this one not in a vehicle.

"And I didn't even know we were going to have a party," she gasped as she sank in shock into the comfy couch under the window she'd been looking through.

Bud turned just as the wild man opened the door and walked in, unannounced and without ringing the doorbell—bare feet, tangled hair, and all.

CHAPTER 36

Bud had never read an Agatha Christie mystery, but he'd seen a couple of them on television, and he knew one of the writer's hallmark techniques was to gather all the murder suspects in one room, where the detective then announced the guilty party, who then explains all.

Bud could see all the suspects were here at the Turner's except Bodie, but he still wasn't entirely sure who had killed Mack Murphy, though he had his suspicions. He guessed Christie was much better at this than he was, even though his cases were real and hers were fiction.

Right now, everyone was watching Tom Turner imitate a Roy Rogers act, and even the wild man Jerry, who had heard the gunshots and come to investigate, was having fun, from the look on his face. He seemed oblivious to the sidelong glances the rest were giving him as he carefully sipped the expensive wine Susie had given him, holding his little finger out as if he were drinking with the Queen of England.

It was an incongruous sight, Bud thought, the scruffy unkempt man with no shoes drinking from a crystal goblet in the expensive well-kept and well-heeled Turner mansion.

Tom now threw his pistol in the air where it twirled a few times on its way down and landed perfectly in the inlaid holster on his hip. The small group cheered as Susie refilled their wine glasses.

Susie was no dummy and was effectively defusing a tense situation, Bud thought. He wondered how it had played out—if Annie had run from the car directly into the house with Boonie right behind her, and how the Turners had dealt with it all. Indie must've already been there, he figured, which would've helped the situation.

Now Tom was inviting everyone to stay for a big barbecue, his specialty, and Susie was yet again refilling the wine glasses. Annie was sitting next to Indie, with Boonie standing on Indie's other side, looking like he'd forgotten his mission to catch Annie. He was now completely enthralled with Tom's gunslinger act.

Carl and Jimmy were eyeing the paper-mache cowheads and looking generally incredulous at the house and its furnishings. It would be something for them to aspire to someday, Bud figured, with their newfound uranium riches.

Now someone else was at the door, and Susie soon led Bodie in and handed him a glass of wine. He had also heard the shots and come to see what was going on. Bodie tried to decline the drink, but Susie would have none of it, telling him she'd gone all the way to Tuscany to get this special cabernet sauvignon for her guests.

Now all the suspects were here, Bud thought, but he had no idea what to do with that. Maybe things would be clearer if he had a glass of wine, and he sure could use some good barbecue—he felt like he'd been starving ever since he came to the valley, excepting the one meal he'd had here with the Turners. That was probably the only reason he was still alive, he figured.

The barbecue was a big success, and though it seemed like an unlikely mix of people to Bud, everyone seemed to be having a great time.

Jerry was having a conversation with Tom about riding the rails, and Bud figured it wouldn't be long until Tom invited the wild man for a ride on his train, from the enthralled look on his face.

Carl and Jimmy were discussing how to make dandelion wine with Susie, who was making a list of the things she would need to do this.

Indie was telling Boonie how to use crop circle cards as a divination tool for facilitating self-awareness through higher frequencies, and Boonie was asking questions about if one could make money doing this. He seemed to have completely forgotten Annie.

Bodie and Annie were back in the corner where Annie could keep an eye on Boonie while Bodie asked her questions about her recent adventure up on the plateau.

Everyone was here, Bud noted with surprise, all the suspects in Mack's murder. He decided it was time for his Agatha Christie ploy. He stood on the base of the big fireplace and whistled, getting everyone's attention.

"Folks, I'm really glad you're all here today, because first of all, it's been a lot of fun, but secondly, it's going to save me a lot of time and running around trying to talk to each one of you individually, and I'm about out of gas.

Jimmy, Carl, and Susie, you can all relax, because none of this pertains to you, but as you may know, the rest of you are all prime suspects in the murder of Mack Murphy.

There's only one suspect missing, and we'll get to him later."

He paused as everyone began talking at once. He waited for them to settle down, then continued.

"I'm going to go through my mental list one by one, and you can all serve as judge and jury for each other. We'll get to the bottom of everything right here and now and save the State of Colorado all that money they'd be out if we did it the formal way over in the Montrose courthouse. This is how Paradox used to mete out justice back in its Wild West days, and it should work just as well now, if you'll all cooperate."

As he spoke, Bud carefully watched everyone's faces. Jimmy and Carl had stepped back a bit and looked a little paranoid, but everyone else looked shocked and like rabbits in headlights. The wine was helping keep everyone subdued, for which Bud was glad. He continued.

"Let's start first with our good host, Tom. Now, Tom, we all know you had good motive to kill Mack."

Susie gasped, and Tom looked annoyed but said nothing. Bud continued.

"Mack and you didn't get along one bit, did you? In fact, it went beyond that—you had some kind of rivalry going to see who could outdo the other in terms of showcase ranches. You even competed in the way you dressed. Mack hated your train, and you hated his buffalo. You could easily have murdered him when you heard him and Indie arguing that night, slinking over there and whacking him on the head when he came outside. Nobody would see you and be any the wiser. You'd be able to pocket the money he'd paid you for your place, and I'm sure it was a significant amount, while then negotiating to buy it back from Annie for a much lesser amount, as you knew she didn't want to be here and would sell cheap. You stood to make quite a bit out of a deal like that, and you even had the kids here looking for gold for you, just so you could one-up Mack, as you sure don't need the money."

Tom was turning red and trying to protest, but Bud just ignored him and continued on.

"Let's move on. Jerry, you're next."

The wild man gave Bud a look that said if he weren't so happily full of barbecue beef and wine, he might have to run off and hide, but he stayed put.

"Jerry, you also had a motive to kill Mack, though it's simpler than Tom's. Mack had come up onto the plateau and totally disregarded the fact that he was on your legal mining claim, then he agreed to pay you off for building his Ute burials there, but then reneged on the deal. When you called him on it, he told you to come work for him, and then reneged on that deal, too, even though it was because he was dead. There's only so much a man can take, especially when he's hungry and depending on someone for groceries who's undependable, isn't that right?"

Bud then added as an aside, "By the way, I have the groceries I promised you out in my FJ, and I'll leave them where I said."

Jerry looked uncomfortable but not very afraid. In fact, Bud thought he looked a bit amused. Bud continued.

"Boonie, you're next. You probably have the least compelling motive to have killed Mack, but it's still possible you did it, and for the same reasons as Jerry. Mack had hired you to work for him, got your hopes up that things might not be so lean up there on the plateau for you for once, then he shut it all down, totally reneged on the deal.

Just like with Jerry, when you live on the edge things like this can make you pretty mad—mad enough to kill, right?"

Jerry started to mutter something, but Bud cut him off.

"And now you're trying to kill Annie because she stole your traps and guns, aren't you?"

Annie held her hand over her mouth, looking panicked.

"It's OK, Annie, those traps are illegal, and I'm not sure how illegal it is to steal something that's illegal, but Boonie never registered them, and they're also leg-hold traps, which have been outlawed in Colorado for a number of years. And I would suspect neither gun is registered. I'm going to confiscate the whole lot and turn it in to the San Miguel County Sheriff, although I may conveniently forget who they belong to, if Boonie cooperates. And I know you took them because he was killing innocent animals, didn't you, Annie? But let's move along."

"Indie, you're next. You and Mack were close, and you knew he had put you in his will, didn't you?"

Indie's eyes flashed as she shouted "No, no, I didn't!" Annie looked shocked, and Bud continued.

"Mack left you the house and Annie's art studio and a few acres of land. Sorry to break the news like this Annie, but I just read his will—you got nothing in Paradox, though plenty elsewhere. Anyway, Indie, you were Mack's advisor, and you knew you stood to gain big with him dead and you in his will. You stood to gain a lot with him gone, and your Hottentot spear would be handy for that. It was easy to kill him after your big argument with him, wasn't it? He never suspected you would do something like that, especially hitting him from behind."

Indie gasped and sank into the chair behind her. She looked like she was ready to cry.

"Annie and Bodie, you're next. Annie, I don't believe you killed Mack personally, but rather hired Bodie here to do your dirty work for you."

Bodie cringed and stepped back a bit, leaning against a bookcase full of limited editions of Sherlock Holmes books bound in leather with inlaid gold titles.

"You're both prime suspects, as I'm sure you know. Bodie, you hated Mack for the way he was making Annie unhappy, a woman you admired and felt protective of. When she came to you and asked you to help her kill Mack, you didn't hesitate. With Mack gone, she would be free to leave the valley and be wealthy enough to go wherever she wanted. She promised to share some of that wealth with you, didn't she, Bodie? I happen to know for a fact that you were the one who took his body to the river, as I saw you both coming and going from the window in Junior's general store."

Bud was just bluffing. In fact, he didn't know anything for a fact. He wasn't even sure what had prompted him to ruin the party like this, but he was frustrated and wanted answers and it looked like a good opportunity to confront everyone and see who blinked first.

He stopped and eyed Bodie and Annie. Bodie was white as a sheet, and as some great writer once said, the tension in the room was palpable.

Bud had never been the center of attention like this, and his nature was to be a reclusive melon farmer, so he wasn't really enjoying it. But he now understood what drew people to acting—the drama and ability to run the show.

But this had indeed been just an act, for he knew who had killed Mack Murphy, and it wasn't anyone in this room.

CHAPTER 37

Bud stood on the fireplace base, completely out of steam, and it seemed like everyone in the room was glaring at him. He wondered if he shouldn't now skulk away, or if he should finish his drama the way it should be done, with full closure. Agatha Christie would have done the latter, but she was a first-rate detective writer, and Bud was just a lowly melon farmer. Maybe he should read one of her books to see how it was really done, he thought.

Nobody was coming forth to state that Bud was right in his assessment of their character, that they had indeed killed Mack Murphy. In fact, everyone seemed even more reticent and unlikely to admit anything than before. The effects of the wine seemed to have quickly dissipated.

Bud walked over to the big picture window, twirling the ends of his mustache, thinking. He knew what he now needed to do, but there were still some loose ends he needed to tie up, and he wasn't sure how to do that. He had kind of walked himself into a corner. He decided to continue.

"Now that you're all stirred up, let this be a reminder to you that we all have flaws and are capable of things we might not want to be capable of. And thank you for humoring me. This has been a tough case, as I had reasons to suspect each of you, as you now know.

"But if everyone wants to come over to this window, I'll show you who that one missing suspect is, the one who actually killed Mack, and paradoxically, the only one with no motive to do so."

They all looked surprised, but came to the window.

Bud pointed over to the buffalo herd.

"See that big bull buffalo over there, the one under the tree? That's who killed Mack Murphy.

"I found the tip of the animal's horn over by Mack's house. I called the coroner, and it fits the wound perfectly. The coroner had measured it and everything, and the horn tip was exactly the right size and dimensions. The bull must've caught Mack right at the base of his neck with it, then the tip came out when it broke off. Mack had argued with Indie, then gone outside when he heard howling, unaware that the buffalo were out and stampeding."

Now everyone was talking at once, and Bud felt the tension lift. He continued.

"I still need to know who took Mack's body to the river, but I think I already do, and if you want to come forward, come by the store and we'll talk about it. At this point, you'll face criminal charges of tampering with evidence and a few other things, but I know Sheriff Masters will be lenient and advise the judge to do the same if you come forward on your own. I personally know exactly why you did it, and I might have even done the same thing, given the circumstances. But it's always best to obey the law."

Bud noticed that both Boonie and Jerry nodded knowingly to each other. They obeyed the law only when they found it prudent to do so, and they weren't very susceptible to what they considered Bud's propaganda. He knew that Carl and Jimmy were also in that same camp—after all, this was the Paradox Valley, where the Wild West lived on in people's minds and in Tom Turner's living room.

Now Susie was pouring more wine, and everyone had relaxed and were asking Bud and each other endless questions. Boonie was following Indie around and seemed to have completely forgotten he was mad at Annie. Tom had brought Maggie into the house and was feeding her barbecue scraps.

Bud decided it was time to go. He felt deflated and tired, and his feet hurt. He thanked Tom and Susie for their hospitality, then walked out the big front door.

As he opened his FJ door, he noticed that someone had followed him out. He turned to see who it was—it was Bodie.

"Wait a minute, Bud," Bodie said, still white as a sheet. "You're right, I'm the one who dumped Mack's body in the river. I'm sorry for that, but at the time, it seemed the thing to do. I honestly thought Annie had killed him. Mack didn't always treat her very nice, and in my mind, at least at the time, killing him in a moment of passion would be understandable. I had no idea a buffalo had gored him. I was trying to protect Annie, and I guess I stupidly figured nobody would find him in the river."

"I understand, Bodie," Bud replied. "I'm not going to arrest you, but will leave it to Sheriff Masters to decide what to do. I know he'll have to charge you with something, but maybe it won't be too bad. Fessing up is the honorable thing to do."

"Annie already told me she'd get me the best attorney around and pay for it. You know, Bud, I love Annie, not like a girlfriend, but rather like you would love someone who has the best heart you've ever known. She reminds me a bit of my mom. Annie just now told me she's going to move to the land she and Mack have up near Flathead Lake in Montana and build a nice house. She wants me to come along and help her build it, as well as take care of the horses. I hope the law will let me. You know, Annie told me she had thought this was all my doing, that I'd started the whole mess by inspiring Mack to want to be like me, a Westerner. I don't know how many evenings I spent over on their big porch telling Mack stories, and it wasn't long after that he changed his name from Rudolf and wanted to be a cowboy. But I didn't do anything intentionally."

"We're all responsible for our own actions, Bodie. She was just looking for answers and that was a handy one, though not very realistic. I'm sure it will all work out. But I thought Annie wanted to go back to California."

"She did until all this happened, and I think it made her see things differently. California's too crowded, and I think she now wants to make a new start somewhere else. She loves nature, and they have 200 acres up there in the big timber with great views of the lake and the Swan Mountains. I've seen photos of it. She wants to start a refuge there for abused horses."

"Bodie, tell Annie that Mack really did love her. He must have, given what he's done."

"How so?"

"He had given up on making the valley into a Wild West theme park. He deeded the entire place to the Audubon Society as a bird sanctuary. I read the contract, and everything's spelled out. The Turner mansion will be the headquarters and main exhibit building. Part of the fields will be converted into native plants, just like he had Jerry do in the one where he's camped. In fact, he even wanted you to stay and work on it, as well as Jerry. He made the Society put in the contract that you were both to be employed as long as you wanted, and he left them a trust fund to pay you from. He thought Jerry would make a great tour guide."

Bodie laughed. "He did? I'll be darned. You know, Jerry does have a presence about him. He'll get himself cleaned up and make a great guide. He knows the plateau and valley like no one on earth. People won't forget him—he'll be an attraction all on his own, the resident Bigfoot."

Bud grinned, then replied, "And Bodie, Mack left the main house and studio to Indie because he wanted her to turn it into a place of refuge for people with problems."

"Well, I guess that was a nice gesture on his part. And I bet she has Boonie working there before you can say siccum."

Bud grinned, then said goodbye to Bodie, who went back into the house, where it sounded like the party was winding up again. Bud then noticed Tom and Jerry were boarding the train, ready to go on a little tour of the ranch, with Carl and Jimmy in the car behind them.

Bud still had a few questions he needed answered, but he was tired. He would drop Jerry's groceries off, then drive on over to Naturita and get gas. He'd then go back to the store and call Wilma Jean to tell her he'd be coming home soon.

CHAPTER 38

Bud was on his way back from Naturita, where he'd gassed up and bought an Eskimo Pie at the little grocery store there, when he decided to swing by the old hot springs and see if Annie was around. He still had some loose ends he wanted to tie up, and he figured only Annie could do that for him.

He wondered what the Audubon Society would do with the old hot springs buildings—maybe turn them into a refuge for tropical water birds, who knows, but more likely tear it down.

Sure enough, Annie's green Subaru was parked in front, now that she no longer needed to hide from Boonie. She was loading up her stuff and seemed surprised to see him.

Bud got out, and Maggie jumped up on him wanting to be petted. Bud stroked her silky ears.

"So, you're heading back to the ranch, I take it?" Bud asked.

"Yes, but only until this thing with Bodie is cleared up, then we're moving to Montana. Carl and Jimmy are going to help us out and drive the moving van. Do you think they'll throw Bodie in jail?"

"No, I doubt it very much, Annie," Bud replied. "I think he'll be charged and released on some kind of small bond, then he'll have to show up in court, but they'll do a plea bargain, since it's his first offense. We'll work it all out."

"I hope you're right," Annie sighed.

"Since he works for you, he technically didn't steal the backhoe, unless you want to press charges on him for putting it in the river."

Annie replied, "No, no need to do that."

"Annie, do you mind if I ask a few questions to tie up some loose ends on the case? Sheriff Masters will be here in a bit to talk it all over, and I want to know exactly what happened. There are a few things I can't figure out."

"Sure, I don't mind."

"What happened that night when Mack was killed? I know he and Indie had been arguing and something stampeded the buffalo with its howling, but what did you do? How did you get out of there and why?"

Annie sighed and leaned against her car. "It was a bad night for me, something I just want to forget. I heard the arguing, and I panicked. Mack had told me he'd rather see me gone than staying in Paradox when I hated it so much, and for some reason I interpreted that as him threatening me. That shows you my state of mind. I was very upset.

"So, when I heard all the yelling going on, I slipped over and opened the wire gate just in case I decided to leave, then went back to Indie's to think. I wanted to sneak off on horseback, and that's why I opened the gate—I didn't want Mack coming after me, and he would hear the car. Indie showed up and told me Mack was furious. I had no idea he had already deeded the place to the Audubon Society and was mad because I refused to talk to him about it. I was going to spend the night at Indie's. I know now he wanted to tell me about his surprise and I ruined all that by refusing to talk to him. He must have felt terrible.

"Anyway, I grabbed my coat and stuffed a few things into a small pack and went and got Kashi, my mare, and slipped her bridle on. Maggie followed me, even though I wanted her to stay with Indie. I jumped on Kashi bareback and took off, not wanting Mack to see me.

"Just then, the howling started in and the other horses panicked and broke out and followed me. Since the gate was already open, we all just thundered out. I was planning on riding down the valley a ways and maybe spending the night at LuAnn's or going over to Junior's, but the horses had other ideas.

"They took off up the rim trail, and there was just enough moonlight that we didn't all get killed. They were totally out of control from the howling. So I went on up to one of our line camps and hid out, putting the horses in the corral where they had grass and water. I had no idea Mack had been killed.

"The next day, I was still really shook up, and I decided to stay up there for awhile and let Mack calm down. But the Bigfoot thing came by and scared me to death that next night, so I went up to the Ute Tower, thinking Maggie and I would be safer there. The day you came up, the howling scared the horses so bad they broke out and took off, and I knew I had to leave, too, so I followed them down the trail.

"You know the rest of the story after that. Indie says that we have to try to love our dark sides, and there's no such thing as Bigfoot. She says it's just my inner beast seeking to be set free, but I was pretty sure it existed when it followed me down the trail."

"Mine must be wanting to be set free, too, cause I heard that thing also," Bud replied. "But Annie, why did you write, 'How could I possibly kill my own husband?' in your notebook? That really led me to think that maybe you had killed Mack, even though I didn't think you had it in you to kill anyone."

"Yeah, that was a dumb thing to write down, I can see that now, but I never suspected anyone would see it. See, Indie had been trying to help me, to get me to let my anger and emotions out more, and she said journaling would be a good way to do that. So, I was really mad at Mack at that point. I felt like he was running roughshod over not just me, but everyone in the valley with his Wild West scheme. I was trying to let the anger out, and I was feeling like killing him, but then I stopped and thought about it. There was no way I could kill him. Writing that down made the anger all go away. I should've destroyed it afterwards, though."

Bud smiled.

"I knew you could never kill anyone. But Annie, can I ask you a really big favor? Is there any way you can negate the contract Mack had on the Paradox Cafe? It's not in the list of Mack's assets in the will, and LuAnn told me it had been postdated, so that's probably why. And she hasn't seen any funds from it. I suspect with this new bird sanctuary the valley's going to be wanting a little cafe and general store for the tourists. I think LuAnn and Junior may end up doing really well. Of course, it's up to her, but I suspect she may want to stay since I know Junior is planning on staying."

Annie smiled. "I'd be happy to void it, and it's probably not legally binding anymore anyway. It's probably in Mack's desk. I'll find it and talk to her. It's the least I can do. LuAnn's a real gem, and I'd hate to see her leave, even though I won't be here. But I'll be back to visit."

Bud thanked her and turned to leave, wondering if Lu-Ann would ever come back to reopen the Paradox Cafe or if Annie's favor would be for naught. He hoped she would return.

CHAPTER 39

Bud had pulled off his boots and set them on the window-sill to dry out, as they were still a bit damp from walking through the ditches in the bird field. He then kicked back and sipped the cup of coffee he'd just made.

He had called Sheriff Joe Masters and told him all the details of the case, and now things were wrapping up. He was anxious to see Wilma Jean and the dogs and be back in his old familiar environment. Besides, it was time to get going on the spring farming, getting the melon fields ready for planting.

He sat back, wondering where Junior was and if he was still in jail. Bud hated to call Howie to find out, as he wasn't in the mood to get involved in a long drawn-out conversation. He'd try calling Wilma Jean soon, he decided, right after he relaxed a bit. It had been a long day.

Bud had just leaned back on Junior's old rickety couch and nodded off when he was startled back awake by some-one downstairs in the store, someone singing the lyrics to "King of the Road" a bit off-key, and it sounded just like his Uncle Junior. And not only that, he thought he could hear Pierre barking.

He must have been dreaming, he figured, getting up and looking out the window. But sure enough, right there in the drive, between his FJ and Junior's old pickup, sat Wilma Jean's pink Lincoln Continental, and leaning against it was Wilma Jean herself. And to make things even more interesting, she was talking to LuAnn! Bud couldn't believe his eyes.

He didn't even bother to slip on his boots, but ran downstairs in his socks, slipping on the bottom stair but managing to catch himself on the edge of the empty ice cream cooler.

"It's a fine thing when you leave your store in someone else's care and they eat everything in it," Junior grinned.

"I gotta pay myself in something," Bud replied, "since the owner forgot to send me any wages."

Bud gave his uncle a big hug. "And you forgot to tell me how to reorder all this stuff. We've been out of Eskimo Pies forever and there's about to be an insurrection here in the valley. I mean, the mayor promises Eskimo Pies if he's elected, then disappears and reneges on the deal. People are getting upset."

Junior laughed just as LuAnn and Wilma Jean walked in, the dogs at their heels. Pierre grabbed onto Bud's pant cuffs while Hoppie barked madly.

Wilma Jean gave Bud a big hug, and LuAnn smiled and made a comment about how he looked like he'd lost a little weight.

"I've been really worried," Bud told Wilma Jean. "Howie said you were changing the menu at the cafe to Chinese. Is that true?"

She laughed. "No, we did that as a diversion so we had an excuse to go up and rescue Junior. We didn't want Howie to head us off at the pass."

"Come on over and I'll open up the cafe and fix every-one something to eat," LuAnn offered. I got some of that good coffee from Salt Lake, and I'll fix a pot."

Bud looked questioningly at his uncle, wondering where LuAnn had come from, but Junior just shrugged his shoulders as if he didn't know either. But after the two women had left, Junior took Bud aside.

"Buddy, my boy, things are looking good. That damn sheriff over there in Emery County, you know, that tall lanky guy that replaced you, well, he threw the book at me, but there's a fine judge over there who tossed the whole thing out. He's a big railroad buff. I invited him to come to the wedding."

"What wedding?"

"What wedding? I asked LuAnn to marry me, and she said yes."

"I thought she proposed to you, and you said no."

"That was all in the past, my boy, before I got cured."

"Cured?"

"Yeah, before Indie cured me. I been seeing her for ad-diction counseling, you know."

"Addiction counseling? What are you addicted to?"

"Was addicted to, Buddy my boy, past tense. I was ad-dicted to my freedom, but Indie made me see that riding the rails wasn't something I wanted to do anymore, and I no longer needed to be afraid of being committed."

"Seems to me you should worry more about getting committed, Uncle," Bud grinned. "And getting thrown in jail sure isn't conducive to freedom."

"I know, I know. But Buddy, that LuAnn, she's a good woman—she managed to track me down, and she and Maureen and your wife talked Judge Richter into dropping everything, though it wasn't hard to do, as he's now a big fan of mine. He promised to not only come to the wedding, but he bought us tickets to ride Amtrak up to Salt Lake for our honeymoon."

"Did LuAnn think this was a good idea?"

"Oh, you bet, and she might even go for a ride on a caboose with us. Richter has a friend who's an engineer up there on a big cannonball and he said we could be freelance passengers for the day. And by the way, that skinny deputy of yours is gonna play for the wedding."

"Howie and the Ramblin' Road Rangers are playing here in Paradox?"

"Yup, and he said Indie said we could have it at her place, out on her lawn. So we're getting hitched tomorrow night. You're gonna do the honors since you're a deputy, the closest thing to mayor here, since I can't do it myself. Indie's going to do a big tofu thingy for the hippies and Tom's doing a barbecue for the rest of us normal folks. No point in waiting around until everyone in the valley's gone. And Tom told me you figured out who killed Mack and it wasn't anybody I know. I bet it was that wild man, wasn't it? Just who was it, anyway?"

Bud laughed as they entered the cafe, Pierre dragging along holding onto his pant cuffs while Hoppie continued to bark. Wilma Jean and LuAnn were already in the kitchen fixing dinner.

As they sat down, Junior said, "I sure appreciate you minding the store for me. It was supposed to only be for a day, but things got a little complicated. I brought you a little present."

Junior dug something from his inside jacket pocket and handed it to Bud.

Bud grinned. It was a box of crayons and a Scooby Doo coloring book.

CHAPTER 40

Bud had just pronounced Angus Fergus O'Connor the Third and LuAnn Elizabeth Luttrell husband and wife and was ready to step down from the stone patio at Indie's, job done, when Junior informed him he wasn't finished, that there was another couple who wanted to get married.

Junior had been a bit late to the wedding, having unexpectedly run out of gas in his old pickup, but fortunately he only had to walk about a half mile, so LuAnn hadn't really had time to panic too much. But because of this, he hadn't been able to warn Bud ahead of time that he was going to perform two weddings, not just one.

This was news to Bud, and he couldn't imagine who it could be until Howie and Maureen walked onto the patio, hand in hand, beaming like newlyweds, dressed in their glittery band costumes, which reminded Bud of something from the Grand Old Opry. They'd decided to get remarried, and they wanted Bud to perform the ceremony.

Bud was wearing his best and only suit, which Wilma Jean had brought from home, although she'd forgotten his dress shoes, so he was wearing his soggy Herman Survivors. But it didn't matter, as most of the crowd was dressed casual, except the brides and grooms. Bud had never seen his uncle in a suit, and he had to admit he looked pretty natty, not at all like a former railroad hobo.

Howie looked nervous as if he'd never done all this before, and Maureen kept giggling at him, but they made it through the ceremony, whereupon Maureen threw her bridal bouquet high into the air.

LuAnn's had been caught by Annie, who smiled like a teenage girl when Bodie grabbed her by the hand to congratulate her, and Bud suspected their friendship might some day become something more serious.

But Maureen's bouquet was caught by Jerry, which everyone thought was hilarious except Jerry, who looked completely embarrassed. He had somehow found a nice shirt and pair of jeans to wear and was even wearing a pair of sandals that seemed to fit. Bud wondered if he hadn't made them himself.

Now Bud remembered the cigars he'd put in his pocket for Boonie what seemed like ages ago. He handed them to Jerry, who grinned like he'd just been given a million dollars. Bud wished he himself were that easily pleased.

Now it was time for the reception, and Indie announced the dinner would begin in fifteen minutes, followed by music and dancing to the infamous Ramblin' Road Rangers from Green River, Utah.

This brought a round of cheering, and Bud noticed his uncle's Noble steel-guitar case sitting by the band's equipment. He hoped Junior was going to play, as he'd never seen him play before.

As Bud and Wilma Jean found seats at a table across from Junior and LuAnn, Jerry came and leaned down next to Junior, putting his hand on his shoulder. This made

Junior jump a bit, as he wasn't used to being around a guy who could easily pass for a Bigfoot in the dark, especially one who had conked him on the head.

Bud couldn't hear what Jerry was saying to Junior, but from the look on Junior's face, he suspected he was apologizing for hitting him and asking if he could somehow make it up. Junior looked serious and was kind of nodding his head yes as he rubbed his head, then he would listen some more as Jerry continued. Suddenly, he jumped from his seat and started whooping and hollering, pounding Jerry on the back.

Now Bud could easily hear what Junior was saying.

"Why you old road bum, I thought there was something familiar about you. Don't tell me you're the guy I rode that black snake with back in the winter from hell. You saved my life, and I'll never forget it!"

Bud knew a black snake was a train made up of coal cars, but he had no idea what the winter from hell referred to—he'd have to ask his uncle what had happened.

After dinner, Howie, Maureen, and Barry all came onto the makeshift stage out under the stars. They had set up flashing strobe lights and a smoke-making machine they'd ordered on the internet from a defunct disco, and even though it was a bit unusual for a country-swing band, the crowd loved it and cheered.

Howie picked up the microphone and thanked everyone for being there. He then announced their first song, something about a runaway truck and a train meeting at some jinxed intersection. As they played, Bud was pleasantly surprised at how good they were. It looked like Howie's first real gig was going to be a big success.

After a short intermission, Howie invited Junior to come up and play his steel guitar with them. Junior had changed out of his suit and back into his Wranglers and red-white-and-blue-striped American flag suspenders and moccasins. They played a few songs, including the Orange Blossom Special, which left everyone dancing and hooting.

Wilma Jean wanted to dance a bit, but Bud's feet were still sore, so he didn't last long, and she ended up dancing a few songs with Judge Richter. Every time the judge danced near the band, Junior made his steel guitar sound like a railroad whistle, which made everyone laugh.

Soon things began to wind down. Bud had really enjoyed the party, but it was now late, and most everyone was gone except for a few who were now in Indie's house, including Indie, Wilma Jean, LuAnn, Junior, the judge, and Jerry. The Turners had gone on home, and Annie and Bodie had also left, going to the nearby ranch house.

As he turned to go inside, Bud first stopped for a moment to listen to the night sounds. An owl hooted in a nearby tree, and the lights at Tom and Susie's across the way shone like bright stars in the thick darkness of the night. Bud knew the couple would soon be on their way to a new life somewhere else, like most everyone else in the valley.

As he grabbed the door handle, he paused. He thought he'd heard a mournful howling in the far distance, maybe from up on the rim high above. It made him shiver a bit, and he knew he'd be glad to get back to his and Wilma Jean's little bungalow at the edge of the melon fields in Green River. It was a long drive, but he wanted to get there tonight.

It was time to go home, back to what he knew and loved best. He went inside and got Wilma Jean, saying his fare-wells to everyone.

They both walked out the door and on to better things.

About the Author

Chinle Miller writes from southeastern Utah, where she spends most of her time wandering with her dogs. She has a B.A. in Anthropology and an M.A. in Linguistics and is currently working on a degree in geology.

If you enjoyed this book, you'll also enjoy the first book in the Bud Shumway mystery series, *The Ghost Rock Cafe*, as well as the second, *The Slickrock Cafe*. And don't miss *Desert Rats: Adventures in the American Outback* and *Uranium Daughter*, both by Chinle Miller.

And if you enjoy Bigfoot stories, you'll love *Rusty Wilson's Bigfoot Campfire Stories* and his many other Bigfoot books, available in paperback or as ebooks from yellowcatbooks.com and your favorite online retailer.

You can also find unique Bigfoot hats and apparel at yellowcatbooks.com.

34486975R00129

Made in the USA
Middletown, DE
23 August 2016